Acting Edition

I0591870

Hooded, or Being Black for Dummies

by Tearrance Arvelle Chisholm

SAMUEL FRENCH

FOR PRODUCTION INQUIRIES

UNITED STATES AND CANADA
info@concordtheatricals.com
1-866-979-0447

UNITED KINGDOM AND EUROPE
licensing@concordtheatricals.co.uk
020-7054-7200

Each title is subject to availability from Concord Theatricals Corp.,
depending upon country of performance. Please be aware that
HOODED, OR BEING BLACK FOR DUMMIES may not be licensed by
Concord Theatricals Corp. in your territory. Professional and amateur
producers should contact the nearest Concord Theatricals Corp. office
or licensing partner to verify availability.

No one shall make any changes in this title(s) for the purpose of production. No part of this book may be reproduced, stored in a retrieval system, scanned, uploaded, or transmitted in any form, by any means, now known or yet to be invented, including mechanical, electronic, digital, photocopying, recording, videotaping, or otherwise, without the prior written permission of the publisher. No one shall share this title(s), or any part of this title(s), through any social media or file hosting websites.

For all inquiries regarding motion picture, television, online/digital and other media rights, please contact Concord Theatricals Corp.

MUSIC AND THIRD-PARTY MATERIALS USE NOTE

Licensees are solely responsible for obtaining formal written permission from copyright owners to use copyrighted music and/or other copyrighted third-party materials (e.g., artworks, logos) in the performance of this play and are strongly cautioned to do so. If no such permission is obtained by the licensee, then the licensee must use only original music and materials that the licensee owns and controls. Licensees are solely responsible and liable for clearances of all third-party copyrighted materials, including without limitation music, and shall indemnify the copyright owners of the play(s) and their licensing agent, Concord Theatricals Corp., against any costs, expenses, losses and liabilities arising from the use of such copyrighted third-party materials by licensees. For music, please contact the appropriate music licensing authority in your territory for the rights to any incidental music.

IMPORTANT BILLING AND CREDIT REQUIREMENTS

If you have obtained performance rights to this title, please refer to your licensing agreement for important billing and credit requirements.

CHARACTERS

The Children

MARQUIS – 14, male, Black

TRU – 14, male, Black

HUNTER – 14, male, White

FIELDER – 14, male, White

CLEMENTINE – 14, female, White

PRAIRIE – 14, female, White

MEADOW – 14, female, White

NEW BLACK KID – 14, male, Black

The Adults

OFFICER BORZOI – male, Black

DEBRA – Marquis' mother, female, White

HEADMASTER BURNS – male, White

APOLLO – male, Black

DIONYSUS – male, White

CONCERNED CITIZEN – male, White

The play requires a minimum of eight actors (three Black males, two White males, three White females) with the following suggested casting:

MARQUIS / NEW BLACK KID
TRU
OFFICER BORZOI / APOLLO
CLEMENTINE
MEADOW
PRAIRIE / DEBRA
HUNTER / HEADMASTER BURNS
FIELDER / DIONYSUS / CONCERNED CITIZEN

Ars Poetica

(Before the play begins, the back wall projects this message:)

"You will be instructed when to laugh. Laughing at any other time makes you a racist."

*(**OFFICER BORZOI** enters with baton and authority.)*

OFFICER BORZOI. Good evening, ladies and gentlemen, welcome to *[name of the theatre]*. Before we begin…

(He removes his cell phone from his hip.)

If you have one of these please take it out now. DO NOT turn it off. DO NOT silence it. On the contrary, please set your ringer to its highest volume. If you're the Dudley Do-Right and have already turned off your cell phone, turn it back on! And set the ringer to its highest volume. This story is unimportant. If your phone rings. Answer it. If you receive a text. Reply. Facebook it. Pin it. Tweet it. Retweet it. Instagram it. Hashtag it. Like it. Love it. – There is no reason to disconnect. Consider this a momentary blip on your living timeline. Keep scrolling.

Noise-making devices, flash photography, video and audio recordings are not discouraged. But I can't fathom why you would want any record of this. Because, as I've said, none of this is important. However, this is: *[additional announcements, emergency exits, etc.]* One last bit of housekeeping: This is the laugh light.

(He gestures toward the laugh light.)

OFFICER BORZOI. It instructs you when to laugh. If the light is on. You laugh. If the light is off. You don't. Laughing when the light is off, make you a racist.

> *(He pauses to make sure no one is laughing. If there is laughter, he admonishes with his baton and authority.)*

Good. I will now return you to your previously scheduled program, already in progress.

> *(He patrols throughout the following scenes. He monitors the audience and their adherence to the laugh light. He reprimands accordingly.)*

A Holding Cell: Stutter 1

(A holding cell: implied bars, a bed/bench, a toilet/sink, a phone.)

(A glass ceiling.)

(The back wall is a projection of a bird's-eye view of the scene within the cell, broadcasting in real time. This shall serve as the backdrop for all the following "stutter" scenes.)

*(**TRU** is sitting on the bench.)*

*(**MARQUIS** is lying face down on the ground. The hood of his sweatshirt is pulled up over his head. Just beyond his hands are a bag of Skittles and an Arizona Sweet Tea.)*

TRU. What was you doin' again?

MARQUIS. Trayvoning.

TRU. …

MARQUIS. You know, it's like Tebowing, or Planking, or Owling.

TRU. …

MARQUIS. You know. It's a meme. Like, you do the thing. Tebowing.

(He Tebows.)

*(**"Laugh"** light on.)*

Owling.

(He owls.)

*(**"Laugh"** light on.)*

Planking.

(He planks.)

*(**"Laugh"** light on.)*

MARQUIS. And there's Plowling. That's when you owl on top of someone planking.

*(**"Laugh"** light on.)*

TRU. Wha's da point?

MARQUIS. You know. You do the thing. And then you take a picture of it and put it up on Facebook or Twitter and you hashtag it. And, like, everybody's doing it, so you're, like, competing to be the most epic at it.

TRU. Whatchu win?

MARQUIS. You don't win anything, per say. It's, like, bragging rights – like, my best friend's older brother once planked on top of a camel in front of the Great Pyramid of Giza. It went viral.

TRU. ...

MARQUIS. Viral. That's, like, when everyone –

TRU. Bruh, I know what viral mean. "Hide ya wife. Hide ya Kids." "Ain't nobody got time fo' dat."* "Momma I love you. P.O.P. Hold me down!"*

*(**"Laugh"** light on.)*

MARQUIS. Right.

TRU. I just don't see da point.

MARQUIS. ...

TRU. So how you, uh...Trayvon?

MARQUIS. You lie down on the ground, in a hoodie, with an Arizona Sweet Tea and a bag of Skittles –

---

*Update with the latest viral catchphrases.

TRU. Like you got shot?

MARQUIS. I guess.

TRU. And why are people doin'nat, yo?

MARQUIS. Planking got old.

(Blackout.)

A Holding Cell: Stutter 2

(Transition: A percussive rap beat being enacted by claps, stomps, and slaps against the chest.)

(Lights go up. **TRU** *is sitting on the bench.* **MARQUIS** *is lying face down on the ground, the hood of his sweatshirt pulled up over his head. Just beyond his hands are a bag of Skittles and an Arizona Sweet Tea.)*

TRU. What was you doin' again?

MARQUIS. Trayvoning.

TRU. And thass illegal?

MARQUIS. No? Not inherently.

TRU. What you get arrested fo' den?

MARQUIS. We were in a cemetery after dark, so technically we were trespassing.

TRU. Who is we?

MARQUIS. My friends and I – Me, Hunter and Fielder.

TRU. *(Like a nerd.)* "Hunter and Fielder"?

MARQUIS. ...

TRU. Dem gotta be some white boys.

MARQUIS. And?

TRU. Dem some white people names, yo. And Trayvonin', das some white people shit.

MARQUIS. It's just a thing.

TRU. A white thing.

MARQUIS. Obviously not. I'm doing it.

TRU. You da only nigga das doin' it too. Voluntarily.

       *("**Laugh**" light on.)*

MARQUIS. What would you rather I do? Some self-serving pseudo-symbol of solidarity? Would you rather I wear my hoodie, with a grave face and my hands up for my profile picture?

TRU. Naw, cuz dat shit is whack too, yo.

       (An impasse.)

Where yo' boys at?

MARQUIS. Who?

TRU. *(Like a nerd.)* "Hunter and Fielder."

MARQUIS. They got away.

TRU. They left da nigga holdin' da bag. Typical.

       *("**Laugh**" light on.)*

MARQUIS. It's not like that. We took off in three different directions. The cop went after me. He could have just as easily gone for them.

TRU. Lemme guess, Officer Borzoi.

MARQUIS. I don't know his name.

TRU. Big. Ugly. Black muthafucka.

MARQUIS. I guess that's him.

TRU. Of course it is, cuz he a ol' Uncle Tommin' ass nigga. He went afta you cuz you was da dark one. He racist.

MARQUIS. How does that even compute? We're the same race.

TRU. Sometimes dem da most racist muthafuckas of 'em all.

       *("**Laugh**" light on.)*

MARQUIS. He was just, like, doing his job.

TRU. Dat muthafucka ain't doin' his job. He wanted to catch you more'n nem. Borzoi singled you out cuz he da worst kinda nigga. Do you know what a Borzoi is?

MARQUIS. No clue.

TRU. It's a breed uh dug – also known as da Russian wolfhound. Know why they call it a wolfhound? Cuz da muthafucka hunt wolf! Ain't dat fucked up? It's a sighthound. Which mean it chase by sight, not by scent. Once he lock eyes on nat wolf he won't stop 'til he hun'it down. Now he oughta see dat wolf as a bruhvuh, but instead he see it as a target. And so he chase it. And when he catch it, he lock hold of dat wolf by da neck and he hold 'em down. He hold dat wolf down by da neck until his master come and slit da wolf throat.

MARQUIS. That's...dark.

TRU. It's a metaphor!

(*Blackout.*)

A Holding Cell: Stutter 3

(Transition: A percussive rap beat being enacted by claps, stomps, and slaps against the chest.)

(Lights go up.)

(TRU *is sitting on the bench.* **MARQUIS** *is lying face down on the ground, the hood of his sweatshirt pulled up over his head. Just beyond his hands are a bag of Skittles and an Arizona Sweet Tea.)*

TRU. What was you doin' again?

MARQUIS. Trayvoning.

TRU. …

MARQUIS. Can I ask you a question?

TRU. Can you?

MARQUIS. How do you know so much about the…Borzoi?

TRU. How come?

MARQUIS. Yeah, why?

TRU. No, how come you wanna know?

MARQUIS. I don't know. I'd never heard of it. I guess it's kind of weird that you –

TRU. That I know somethin' you don't? You think it's weird I can use my head for more'n a hat rack?

MARQUIS. No, I'm not saying that at all –

TRU. I knew it! You a Borzoi too!

MARQUIS. Am not!

*(***"Laugh"*** light on.)*

TRU. Yes you is. I mighta known it too. Look at you. In yo' tie and yo' prep academy sweatshirt, and nem slippery earls –

MARQUIS. Slippery what?

TRU. Earls. Slippery Earls.

MARQUIS. …

TRU. Schwops.

MARQUIS. …

TRU. *(Like a nerd.)* Dress shoes.

MARQUIS. And?

TRU. Who da fuck walk around dressed like dat if they ain't goin' to church…or court. Borzois, das who.

MARQUIS. It's my uniform.

TRU. Fo' what? The Young Republicans Club?

> **(MARQUIS** *averts his eyes.)*

Oh my god. YOU A FUCKIN' REPUBLICAN!

MARQUIS. Look. All I was saying is that it registered as a little strange that you knew so much about some random breed of dog – Not because of who you are, just because it's a really random bit of information.

TRU. Oh. So if "Hunter" started teachin' you 'bout da Rhodesian Ridgeback or if "Fielder" gave you da rundown on da Finnish Spitz, would you think that'd "register as strange"?

MARQUIS. Yes. It would, because Hunter and Fielder are idiots.

> **("Laugh"** *light on.)*

TRU. I really don' feel like I should have to justify why I know somethin'.

MARQUIS. I'm not asking you to –

TRU. But if you really wanna know. I usetuh wanna be a veterinarian when I grew up.

MARQUIS. Used to?

TRU. Yeah. When I was a kid. I usetuh go to da library and I check out all deese books on dugs an' cats an' horses an' shit.

MARQUIS. So you don't want to be a vet anymore?

TRU. No.

MARQUIS. Why not?

TRU. Cuz dat was some shit I thought when I was just a dumb lil' kid, yo.

MARQUIS. So what do you want to be now?

TRU. Alive.

> ("**Laugh**" *light on.*)

MARQUIS. I'm going to be a lawyer.

> ("**Laugh**" *light on.*)

TRU. A lawyer? Really?

MARQUIS. Yes. Once I graduate high school, I'll go to a university. I'll major in Political Science and Philosophy, that way I'll be more well-rounded. I'll work really hard, make the dean's list all four years, and graduate summa cum laude. Then I'll be able to write my ticket to the law school of my choice. That being said, both my parents went to Harvard, so that's where I'm going.

I'll specialize in family law, I'll get my Juris Doctorate degree in three years and I'll start work for a major law firm by the age of twenty-seven.

TRU. Wow.

MARQUIS. What?

TRU. You talk like a white person, yo.

(**"Laugh"** *light on.*)

MARQUIS. Here we go. I hate it when people say that. Just because I use the King's English people say I sound white –

TRU. I ain't talkin' 'bout da "King's English": "For I am quite capable of speaking proper English if I so desire."

MARQUIS. Why don't you?

TRU. I'm talkin' 'bout what you say, not how you say it.

MARQUIS. What did I say?

TRU. All dat shit 'bout, "I'm going to do this," "Then I'll do that." Thass some white people shit, yo!

MARQUIS. …

TRU. Where I'm from, people don' talk like dat. Shit ain't dat sure.

We say "hopefully I can do dis" or "maybe one day I can do dat." Errbody got a dream, an' das all it is. An' it'd be cute if it happen, but we just as prepared for when it don't.

(**"Laugh"** *light on.*)

MARQUIS. That's really messed up.

TRU. It is what it is.

MARQUIS. Maybe if you thought more positively –

TRU. We'd end up more disappointed.

MARQUIS. Dude, like you could totally be a veterinarian. You just have to make a plan, and go after it. I could help you. You're smart –

TRU. I don' need you to tell me I'm smart.

MARQUIS. Dude, I think you do.

(Blackout.)

A Holding Cell: Stutter 4

(Transition: A percussive rap beat being enacted by claps, stomps, and slaps against the chest.)

(Lights go up.)

*(**TRU** is sitting on the bench. **MARQUIS** is lying face down on the ground, the hood of his sweatshirt pulled up over his head. Just beyond his hands are a bag of Skittles and an Arizona Sweet Tea.)*

TRU. What was you doin' again?

MARQUIS. Trayvoning.

TRU. In a cemetery?

MARQUIS. Right.

TRU. Trespassin'?

MARQUIS. Trayvoning while trespassing.

TRU. An' you ran?

MARQUIS. Yes.

TRU. From da police?

MARQUIS. Officer Borzoi, apparently.

TRU. An' you ain't get shot?

*(**"Laugh"** light on.)*

MARQUIS. So what did you do?

TRU. Nothin'.

MARQUIS. You don't get arrested for nothing. I'm sure you were doing something.

TRU. Bein' while black.

MARQUIS. ...

TRU. You ain't gotta be doin' nuffin to attract the attention
uh da police. I got picked up for bein' black at da wrong
place at da wrong time.

>   ("**Laugh**" *light on.*)

>   (MARQUIS *scoffs.*)

MARQUIS. You can't get arrested for that.

>   ("**Laugh**" *light on.*)

>   (TRU *scoffs.*)

TRU. You did.

>   (*Blackout.*)

Debra

(Transition: A percussive rap beat being enacted by claps, stomps, and slaps against the chest.)

*(Suddenly, **DEBRA** enters in a swirl of legal documents.)*

*(She is followed by **OFFICER BORZOI**.)*

DEBRA. I would like to know why Marquis has been arrested!

OFFICER BORZOI. Calm down, ma'am –

DEBRA. Do not tell me to "calm down." I am not uncalm! If you like, I can show you uncalm!

OFFICER BORZOI. He was trespassing ma'am.

DEBRA. Trespassing? Marquis has never been in trouble before. Ever! He's a fourteen-year-old boy, with a bright future ahead of him, and if you think I'm going to allow some frivolous misdemeanor to stand on his record you're dead wrong – and I'll wager I'll have your badge by the end of the hearing. The unlawful arrest and detainment of a minor is not something the Chief of Police takes lightly in his jurisdiction. You know Hal don't you –

OFFICER BORZOI. Yes ma'am, of course.

DEBRA. I'll give him your best when he's over for cocktails this weekend.

OFFICER BORZOI. Listen ma'am, there's no need to get the chief involved. I haven't charged the boy –

DEBRA. Marquis.

OFFICER BORZOI. I haven't charged…Marquis with anything. I simply detained him until he could be released into the custody of his guardian.

DEBRA. Well, I'm here. Albeit a complete waste of my time.

OFFICER BORZOI. I apologize for the inconvenience. Follow me ma'am, and we'll get this taken care of right away.

> *(They exit.)*

TRU. Daaayum! I wish I had a caseworker like dat.

MARQUIS. What are you talking about?

TRU. She was like, "I'ma call da chief of police on yo' monkey ass!" I ain't never seen dat nigga Borzoi look so shook. Gotchu a good one, my caseworker ain't do shit fo' me.

MARQUIS. She's not my caseworker. She's my mother.

TRU. Wait...thass yo muhvuh?

MARQUIS. ...

TRU. I hate to break dis to ya but, dat bitch is white, yo!

MARQUIS. I know she's white! And don't call her a..."B."

TRU. My bad... So what is she, like, albino? Or you jus' got one helluva tan?

MARQUIS. I'm adopted. Okay?

TRU. So dis some *Blind Side*-type shit. Only she ain't as fine as Sandra Bullock, and you ain't nowhere near as big as dat nigga in da movie. They ain't gettin' no football scholarship offa yo' ass.

MARQUIS. It's nothing like that. She's always been my mother.

> *(**OFFICER BORZOI** and **DEBRA** re-enter.)*

DEBRA. I'm glad we could get this taken care of so speedily, Officer Borzoi.

OFFICER BORZOI. Again, I apologize for any inconvenience I may have caused you and your son.

TRU. Ha ha! Listen to dat nigga shuck and jive.

OFFICER BORZOI. Quiet, you little –

DEBRA. And now, why is this young man being held?

OFFICER BORZOI. No need to concern yourself with him ma'am. This one's a bad egg.

DEBRA. What is he being charged with?

OFFICER BORZOI. Ma'am –

DEBRA. What are his charges?

OFFICER BORZOI. Loitering. And disturbing the peace.

DEBRA. Trespassing? Loitering? Has it been a slow night for you Officer Borzoi, or do you have something against young...men, being young men?

OFFICER BORZOI. ...

DEBRA. Release him.

OFFICER BORZOI. No, ma'am. He's truly a bad egg, a bad element. He's been here time and time before. I'm holding him until I can release him into the custody of a guardian.

TRU. But my muhvuh work da graveyard shift –

OFFICER BORZOI. Well then you'll be here until she can make you a priority.

MARQUIS. Can we help him Mom?

DEBRA. Of course we can – Excuse me Officer Borzoi, but you have no right to speak to him that way. His mother is clearly doing the best that she can. She's a single woman, uneducated, living in poverty, working two jobs at minimum wage to make ends meet because she doesn't have a college education.

She's barely got time to think let alone keep tabs on a young, growing boy, who may get into a little trouble every now and again, but it's the only thing he knows.

OFFICER BORZOI. That's all well and good, ma'am, but the law states he can only be released into the custody of a parent or other suitable agency –

DEBRA. Do not quote the law to me Officer Borzoi. I'm a custodian of said law and I am well versed in it. You will release the boy to me as I am his guardian.

OFFICER BORZOI. …

DEBRA. I'm his lawyer.

(Blackout.)

Tupac vs. Nietzsche

(In Marquis' room. Typical suburban teenager's room, except the posters of pop stars are replaced with dead white literary figures. A glass ceiling.)

*(**DEBRA** drops off a stack of starched linens and a couple of sleeping bags.)*

DEBRA. Here, you can shower and sleep in these. And just leave what you're wearing now in a pile by the door. I'll wash it out for you.

TRU. Bet.

DEBRA. I thought you guys could sleep in the sleeping bags. Wouldn't that be fun?

MARQUIS. It'd be fun to sleep in my own bed.

DEBRA. Sleep in the bag with Tru…

TRU. I ain't sharin' no sleepin' bag wit' him.

DEBRA. Not in the same – You'd have your own of course.

*(To **MARQUIS**.)* Marquis, this your first friend to sleep over –

MARQUIS. Hunter and Fielder stay over all the time –

DEBRA. *(To **MARQUIS**.)* Your first "cultural" friend. You wouldn't want to sleep in your bed and make him sleep on the floor. Show him that you two are equals.

MARQUIS. But Mom –

DEBRA. Sleep in the sleeping bags, it'll be like a campout.

TRU. Black people don' camp out.

DEBRA. Where do you get these things? Yes, of course they do. Marquis camps out all the time.

TRU. But he ain't no normal black person.

DEBRA. ...You are a hoot, Tru. You're so full of street sass and moxie.

TRU. I try. I try.

DEBRA. I wish Marquis had a bit of that in him.

MARQUIS. Mom!

DEBRA. I'm sorry, but I do. You can be rather timid at times. Reserved. I wish you had a little more, I don't know...

TRU. Swag. Swag is da word I think you lookin' fo'.

DEBRA. Yes. I wish you had a little more swag.

TRU. Oooohh! Check Moms out! She clowning you, yo!

MARQUIS. Mom! You're embarrassing me.

DEBRA. Bathe. Then get a good night's rest. I'll drive you into the city in the morning.

TRU. Back to Baltimore?

DEBRA. Yes.

TRU. Oh. Okay. Thass fine.

DEBRA. What's the matter?

TRU. Nothin'. No. Thass fine. I'll go home tomorr'.

DEBRA. Tru? What's the matter?

TRU. Nothin'. It's jus dat my muhvuh's workin' two doubles dis weekend...and a couple of singles...she needs da overtime...

DEBRA. Oh god, honey! No. You will stay here, of course. I won't hear another word. You'll call her and let her know where you are so she doesn't worry. She's got enough on her plate just trying to pay the back rent and get the gas turned back on.

TRU. I'll try, but it's hard to catch her between shifts –

DEBRA. Of course. Of course. Well, do your best. And bathe. Good night you two. Try not to stay up too late. Tru, you'll at least shower won't you –

MARQUIS. Thanks, Mom. I think he gets it.

(**DEBRA** *exits.*)

TRU. Why she assume I'm dirty?

MARQUIS. She assumes everything is dirty. Don't take it personally.

(**MARQUIS** *tosses a couple of pillows to* **TRU.***)*

TRU. What deese fo'?

MARQUIS. Those sleeping bags aren't very comfortable.

TRU. Thass aight, cuz I'm sleepin' in da bed.

MARQUIS. No, you're not.

TRU. Sure I am.

MARQUIS. What makes you think you're getting the bed?

TRU. Cuz I'm da guest. And...I ain't got no bed at home. I sleep on da flo'...da cold linoleum-hardwood...with nothin' but a fitted sheet.

(*A beat.*)

MARQUIS. Fine. You can take the bed.

TRU. Thought so. 'Preciate it bruh.

(**TRU** *flops onto Marquis' bed.*)

MARQUIS. Keep your sneakers off the duvet cover, please!

TRU. Sneakuhs? Nigga, do you know what deese are?!

MARQUIS. ...

(**TRU** *holds up his foot, showing of a bejeweled pair of ruby-red Air Jordans.*)

TRU. These are Js. Sevens. Retros. Limited-edition "Dorothies," they only made twenty pair in my size and I camped out all night at Mondawmin Mall to get deese joints.

MARQUIS. I thought black people didn't camp out.

TRU. Fo' a fresh pair uh Js, niggas will shoot they bruhvuh.

MARQUIS. ...

> *(Stalemate.* **TRU** *looks through Marquis' things, surveying his bookshelf.)*

TRU. What da fuck is Nightz-Chee?

MARQUIS. ...

> *(***TRU** *shows him the book.)*

That's Nietzsche. And it's not a what, it's a who. A he. And he happens to be the most brilliant person that ever walked the earth.

TRU. He white?

MARQUIS. What? Why does that even matter?

TRU. He white.

MARQUIS. Whatever. He's brilliant. He had this whole theory about the duality of personality and fragmented consciousness. There's a little bit of Apollo and Dionysus in all of us –

TRU. ...

MARQUIS. Apollo is knowledge. While Dionysus, his brother, is ecstasy. And it's the conflict between these two brothers within us that is the source of everything we do. Here.

(Reads.) "The two creative tendencies developed alongside one another, usually in fierce opposition, each by its taunts forcing the other to more energetic production" – and I can tell by that glassy look in your eyes, that you're completely lost –

TRU. No, I'm completely bored. I understand it doh.

MARQUIS. Oh?

TRU. Yeah. I just don' understand how come he used so many big words to say it. Tupac said the same thing in his poem "Depths of Solitude" –

MARQUIS. Tu-Who?

TRU. You killin' me, Smalls. Tupac Amaru Shakur? 2Pac? Pac? The Great Makaveli!

MARQUIS. Nothing.

TRU. Goddamn, yo! It's worse than I thought. Tupac Amaru Shakur, da greatest rapper uh all time. Baltimore raised. Poet. Actor. Prophet. The original ride or die nigga. Assassinated by haters at da age of twenty-five.

MARQUIS. ...

TRU. He said da same thing this Neetchez guy said. Basically, you can't never be alone cuz there are two people inside of you. And that duo within causes a nigga to live and learn twice as fast –

MARQUIS. I'm sure they aren't talking about the same thing.

TRU. Why not?

MARQUIS. They just weren't okay? Nietzsche was...the truth.

TRU. You wouldn't know true if it was starin' you in da face.

MARQUIS. Is any of that stuff true about your mom working three jobs, and the gas being off?

TRU. I dunno. What do you think?

MARQUIS. I think it could be true. I think that's why you want to stay here. Because you have a dysfunctional home environment?

TRU. I got a dysfunctional home environment? – Nigga, I'm doin' you a favuh.

MARQUIS. Me? You're doing me a favor?

TRU. Sure. I saw you an' said, "Look at dis nigga. He sleep. No swag, whatsoever. His muhvuh a white lady. He ain't got no clue who he really is. And he got a slim chance of ever figurin' it out." I felt sorry fo' you.

MARQUIS. You felt sorry for me? That's rich.

TRU. What's so rich 'bout it?

MARQUIS. Because I feel sorry for you.

TRU. Ain't nobody ask you to feel sorry fo' me.

MARQUIS. But that's all you've been asking me to do since we met. You made us see you as a victim.

TRU. I don' want yo' pity.

MARQUIS. Don't you?

TRU. No!

MARQUIS. Well I do – pity you. Because if all that stuff is true, then that's sad and I feel sorry for you. And if it's not true, and you feel you need to manipulate people, then that's sad too, and I feel sorry for you.

TRU. ...

MARQUIS. Enjoy the bed.

> (**MARQUIS** *settles into the sleeping bag.* **TRU** *reclines on the bed.*)
>
> (*Blackout.*)

Weird Dream

(Marquis' bedroom. The next morning.)

*(**MARQUIS** rises. He sees the lump in his bed.)*

MARQUIS. I had a weird dream.

I was on this floating island with Apollo, the god. He's got this black hood over his head, and he's whispering. He's telling me a secret. My secret. You know how some things in dreams are just understood? It's like that. I know this secret is for me and only me. But he's whispering so low that I have to lean in really close, and just as I begin to understand his tongue rolls out of his mouth and becomes this heavy amber rope. The rope squeezes and chokes me until darkness begins to creep in around the edges of my eyes. But just before I breathe my last breath, Dionysus appears. He's radiant and white with golden leaves in his hair and he grins with his eyes. And I cry because I'm ashamed of the secret that my Apollo gave me. Dionysus tells me to forget it, but I can't. So he cuts a gash in his thigh and sews me inside of it, and he gives birth to me again.

(To the lump in the bed.) Isn't that weird?

...

*(**MARQUIS** pulls back the covers to reveal that the bed is empty.)*

(Blackout.)

The Girls: Stutter 1

(The quad at Achievement Heights Preparatory Academy. Brick and manicured hedges.)

*(**PRAIRIE**, **MEADOW**, and **CLEMENTINE** stand in the foreground. They have their faces in cell phones.)*

*(**MARQUIS**, **HUNTER**, and **FIELDER** stand in the background. They silently vie for the **GIRLS**' attention.)*

*(**OFFICER BORZOI** begins his silent patrol. He holds the audience accountable to the laugh light for the following "stutter" scenes.)*

MEADOW. SELFIE!

*(They all make duck faces for **MEADOW**'s phone. She snaps the picture. They look at it.)*

CLEMENTINE. Cute.

PRAIRIE. Very cute.

MEADOW. Super ca-yute!

Instagram?

PRAIRIE. Totes.

*(**"Laugh"** light on.)*

*(**MEADOW** busies herself with her phone.)*

OMG, Clemie have you seen this? Disney Princesses as Historic Women.

CLEMENTINE. Duh! I'm the one that posted it on your wall.

PRAIRIE. Right. I think Snow White as Anne Frank is my favorite.

CLEMENTINE. I love Belle as Louisa May Alcott. I made it my screen saver. See.

MEADOW. Let me see that...

This is lame. I've never heard of some of these women. And not all of them are even princesses.

CLEMENTINE. Relax. They're in the Disney canon.

MEADOW. Yes, but as a staunch supporter of Disney Princesses I hate it when people improperly attribute the title of "princess" to someone who is NOT a princess.

> (**"Laugh"** *light on.*)

> (**MEADOW** *scrolls.*)

See? Esmerelda, not a princess. Mulan, not a princess. Tiana, not a princess.

CLEMENTINE. She becomes one in the end.

MEADOW. Just barely. And look, they've got her playing Harriet Tub-man. Who the eff is Harriet Tub-man?

CLEMENTINE. Harriet Tubman. She was a slave... Don't you remember anything from Black History Month?

MEADOW. You mean those trivia cards in Civics class?

PRAIRIE. I'm really good at trivia.

> (**"Laugh"** *light on.*)

MEADOW. Is she that woman that couldn't get a seat on the bus...or something?

PRAIRIE. That's Rosa Parks.

CLEMENTINE. Thank you, Prairie.

PRAIRIE. Harriet Tubman owned a railroad.

CLEMENTINE. She didn't own a railroad. She was a conductor on the Underground Railroad.

MEADOW. Like the subway?

PRAIRIE. The last time I was in New York, me and my dad rode the subway "for the culture of it all." It was just crowded and sad. Then this homeless man with mismatched shoes begged me for my leftovers. And then he ate them in front of me.

      ("**Laugh**" *light on.*)

CLEMENTINE. We're not talking about the subway. They didn't have subways back then.

PRAIRIE. Then how did they get the trains underground?

CLEMENTINE. They didn't. There weren't any trains... I don't think.

PRAIRIE. Then why did they call it a railroad?

CLEMENTINE. I don't know.

MEADOW. So you don't know what it is either!

      (*Blackout.*)

The Boys: Stutter 1

(The quad at Achievement Heights Preparatory Academy. Brick and manicured hedges.)

*(**MARQUIS**, **HUNTER**, and **FIELDER** stand in the foreground.)*

*(**PRAIRIE**, **MEADOW**, and **CLEMENTINE** stand in the background. They have their faces in cell phones. They make a great show of being unfazed by the **BOYS**.)*

HUNTER. Dude, I said I was sorry.

FIELDER. So did I.

MARQUIS. That doesn't negate the fact that you both left me…holding the bag.

FIELDER. What bag?

HUNTER. We didn't leave you. We split up.

MARQUIS. You could have done something. Why didn't you call my mom?

HUNTER. Two reasons. One: we didn't know what was going to happen. That cop might have let you go with a warning. And then you would've gotten in trouble unnecessarily.

MARQUIS. And two?

HUNTER. Two: if we'd called your mom, we would have had to admit that we were there with you. And then we would have got in trouble unnecessarily.

MARQUIS. Right.

FIELDER. You didn't tell your mom we were with you, did you?

MARQUIS. Of course not. I'm no rat.

FIELDER. Good. Good. It's a lucky thing it was you who got caught then. My father would have beat me like a slave if I'd gotten arrested.

HUNTER. Dude! He's standing right here.

MARQUIS. ...

FIELDER. Like a Hebrew slave...not like a black one.

*(***"Laugh"*** *light on.)*

MARQUIS. What are you even talking about, Fielder? Your dad is a nice guy.

FIELDER. In public. Remember when we all got detention for cheating on that test?

MARQUIS. I wasn't cheating. You guys were cheating off of me.

FIELDER. Irregardless. You two got off scot-free.

But my dad took me in the basement, stripped me naked, tied me to a board by my wrists and ankles, covered my face with a towel and started pouring water over it.

*(***"Laugh"*** *light on.)*

MARQUIS. What you're describing is waterboarding, and I'm sure that's not true.

FIELDER. He wanted me to tell him it was your fault. That is was your idea.

MARQUIS. Mine?

FIELDER. I lay there while he dumped water over my face and screamed, "Marquis made you do it!" Drown! "Marquis made you do it!" Choke! "He that lies down with dogs shall rise up with Fleas!" Suffocate!

*(***"Laugh"*** *light on.)*

MARQUIS. Did you tell him I made you do it?

FIELDER. Of course I did. I just wanted it to stop.

HUNTER. What happened then?

FIELDER. He forbid me to see you "ever again"... Which reminds me, I'm not even supposed to be talking to you.

(Blackout.)

The Girls: Stutter 2

(The quad at Achievement Heights Preparatory Academy. Brick and manicured hedges.)

*(**PRAIRIE, MEADOW,** and **CLEMENTINE** stand in the foreground. They have their faces in cell phones. **MARQUIS, HUNTER,** and **FIELDER** stand in the background. They silently vie for the **GIRLS'** attention.)*

MEADOW. SELFIE!

*(They all make duck faces for **MEADOW's** phone. She snaps the picture. They look at it.)*

CLEMENTINE. Cute.

PRAIRIE. Very cute.

MEADOW. Super ca-yute!

Instagram?

PRAIRIE. Totes.

*(**CLEMENTINE** reads from her phone.)*

CLEMENTINE. "The Underground Railroad was a network of secret routes and safehouses used by nineteenth-century slaves of African descent in the United States to escape to freedom." So you see, it was a figurative railroad.

MEADOW. Thanks Wikipedia.

PRAIRIE. You know what I never understood about slaves? Like, if they didn't want to be slaves anymore, why didn't they just quit?

*(**"Laugh"** light on.)*

CLEMENTINE. That's not –

MEADOW. Are the boys looking at us?

PRAIRIE. You know they are.

MEADOW. Say-who-you-think-is-the-cutest-on-three! One...two...three!

MEADOW & PRAIRIE. Hunter!

MEADOW. You can't like Hunter! You know I've already confessed my undying love for Hunter.

PRAIRIE. Wait...which one is Hunter?

MEADOW. The jaw.

PRAIRIE. Right. Then I meant Fielder.

MEADOW. ...

PRAIRIE. Really. I get their names confused sometimes, but I definitely meant Fielder. So see, now it's perfect. We've got no competition –

MEADOW. Not so fast. Clementine didn't say.

PRAIRIE. She's right. Clementine, you didn't say.

CLEMENTINE. Don't worry. There's still no competition.

(They think about this.)

PRAIRIE. Wait, what are you saying?

MEADOW. Are you saying you have a crush on Marquis?

PRAIRIE. Are you saying you have a crush on Marquis?

CLEMENTINE. I'm saying...I might.

MEADOW. ...

PRAIRIE. ...

MEADOW. But you don't really like Marquis. Do you?

PRAIRIE. But you don't really like Marquis. Do you?

CLEMENTINE. I think he's really cool.

MEADOW. But you can't like Marquis.

CLEMENTINE. Why not?

MEADOW. Because...

CLEMENTINE. ?

MEADOW. C'mon Prairie, you know why.

PRAIRIE. ?

MEADOW. Do I have to spell it out?

CLEMENTINE. ...

PRAIRIE. ...

MEADOW. You can't like him, because he's...because he's...
ADOPTED!

> (**"Laugh"** *light on.*)

And he just got out of jail. He's an ex-con!

> (*Blackout.*)

The Boys: Stutter 2

*(The quad at Achievement Heights Preparatory
Academy. Brick and manicured hedges.)*

*(MARQUIS, HUNTER, and FIELDER stand in
the foreground.)*

*(PRAIRIE, MEADOW, and CLEMENTINE stand
in the background. They have their faces in
cell phones. They make a great show of being
unfazed by the BOYS.)*

HUNTER. Dude, I said I was sorry.

FIELDER. So did I –

MARQUIS. You can stop apologizing. I'm over it.

FIELDER. I just couldn't get in trouble again. Not with you.
Not with the police. Not with you and the police. That
would have been all bad.

HUNTER. What do you think your dad meant by that dog-
flea thing?

MARQUIS. Let's just drop it, okay?

HUNTER. The thing is though, I would gladly trade places
with either one of you.

MARQUIS. ...

FIELDER. ...

HUNTER. Seriously! Fielder, how badass is it that you can
say you've literally been tortured and survived? And
Marquis, c'mon, if I had gotten arrested my BBQ would
increase exponentially.

MARQUIS. BBQ?

HUNTER. Bad boy quotient.

*("**Laugh**" light on.)*

MARQUIS. I hadn't considered that. I must be the talk of Achievement Prep.

HUNTER. Yeah, but...it had the reverse effect.

MARQUIS. What do you mean?

HUNTER. Well, say it had been me people would see me as a...renegade. A rebel without a cause. Instant cool points. But, and no offense, based on certain stereotypes, which I don't agree with, people sort of expect you to get arrested. So you got tragic points, not cool points.

    ("**Laugh**" *light on.*)

MARQUIS. What do you mean people expect me –

HUNTER. Dude, chillax! Don't be so sensitive.

    (*Blackout.*)

The Girls: Stutter 3

(The quad at Achievement Heights Preparatory Academy. Brick and manicured hedges.)

(PRAIRIE, MEADOW, *and* **CLEMENTINE** *stand in the foreground. They have their faces in cell phones.)*

(MARQUIS, HUNTER, *and* **FIELDER** *stand in the background. They silently vie for the* **GIRLS'** *attention.)*

MEADOW. SELFIE!

(They all make duck faces for **MEADOW**'s *phone. She snaps the picture. They look at it.)*

CLEMENTINE. Cute.

PRAIRIE. Very cute.

MEADOW. Super ca-yute!

Instagram?

PRAIRIE. Totes.

MEADOW. Don't look at me like that. I'm just looking out for your children.

CLEMENTINE. ...

MEADOW. It's like my mom says: halfsies are cute, but they have frizzy hair and personality disorders.

PRAIRIE. OMG...Meadow, are you a racist?

MEADOW. Of course I'm not racist. Both of my parents voted for Hillary.

("**Laugh**" *light on.)*

CLEMENTINE. ...

MEADOW. Stop looking at me like that Clementine. You don't even really like Marquis. You're just saying that because you're in your so-called "rebellious phase." Don't take it too far Miley.

(**PRAIRIE** *twerks.*)

CLEMENTINE. I'm not in any rebellious phase. I think he's cute, and smart, and funny, and –

MEADOW. He's an experiment! You do this all the time. You befriend some outcast to make yourself look all caring and righteous, but it never turns out right. Remember what happened last time? You started pretending to be, like, besties with that girl, Droolia from Special Ed, and what happened to that? She ended up eating your pencil box.

(**PRAIRIE** *laughs.*)

Don't laugh. She almost died.

(**"Laugh"** *light on.*)

CLEMENTINE. That's not fair. Julia and I were close.

MEADOW. You sat close. She didn't even know that you were there half the time. Look, all I'm saying is this is something that you do. You are, like, the patron saint of lost causes.

CLEMENTINE. I am not.

MEADOW. You are too.

CLEMENTINE. Am not!

PRAIRIE. Yeah…you kinda are.

CLEMENTINE. I am not. But even if I was, that isn't what this is.

MEADOW. Then prove it.

CLEMENTINE. Prove it how?

MEADOW. If you're so in love with Marquis, go talk to him.

   (Blackout.)

The Boys: Stutter 3

(The quad at Achievement Heights Preparatory Academy. Brick and manicured hedges.)

*(***MARQUIS, HUNTER,*** and ***FIELDER*** stand in the foreground.)*

*(***PRAIRIE, MEADOW,*** and ***CLEMENTINE*** stand in the background. They have their faces in cell phones. They make a great show of being unfazed by the ***BOYS****.)*

HUNTER. Dude, I said I was sorry.

FIELDER. So did I –

MARQUIS. Let's just drop it. Okay?

HUNTER. Okay.

FIELDER. Okay.

> *(Pause.)*

HUNTER. So what was jail like?

FIELDER. Hunter!

HUNTER. I want to know. Did you get butt raped?

FIELDER. He wasn't there long enough for that. Were you?

MARQUIS. Of course not.

HUNTER. Did you have your own cell, or did they just mix you into gen-pop with the murderers and rapists?

MARQUIS. Gen-pop?

HUNTER. General Population.

MARQUIS. …

FIELDER. …

HUNTER. What? *Lockdown* is my favorite show.

("**Laugh**" *light on.*)

MARQUIS. I didn't go to prison, Hunter. I was at the Achievement Heights municipal police office, in a holding cell, alone. It wasn't a big deal. They didn't even fingerprint me.

FIELDER. No mug shot?

MARQUIS. Not even.

FIELDER. Then it won't be on your permanent record.

MARQUIS. Right. It's like it never happened. So let's just move on!

HUNTER. God, Meadow is so hot! If I had my way, I'd bend her over and...

> (**HUNTER** *makes a series of awkward sexual gestures. He's clearly a virgin.*)

FIELDER. You wouldn't know what to do with her.

HUNTER. But man I'd have fun trying to figure it out. Besides I know more than you fags, at least I've made it to third base before.

FIELDER. Which one is third base again?

MARQUIS. French, feel, finger, "F."

HUNTER. Right, and have you guys ever finger binged somebody? No. I don't think so.

FIELDER. Yeah, but yours was with Droolia.

HUNTER. So? Droolia has huge tits. And she's a freak.

FIELDER. And she's retarded.

HUNTER. Not retarded, "differently abled."

("**Laugh**" *light on.*)

And it doesn't matter, because at the end of the day, I've made it to third base while you guys are still waiting in the dugout. Ha! You guys are still in the locker room… with each other…doing gay stuff.

MARQUIS. I'm in no rush.

HUNTER. Which explains why you haven't made your move on Clementine Perkins. You're afraid of girls.

MARQUIS. Afraid of girls?

HUNTER. Is there an echo?

> (**FIELDER** *laughs.*)

What are you laughing at Fielder? I don't even think you like girls at all.

FIELDER. Shut up! I do like girls. I think about girls all the time.

HUNTER. Yeah. You think about doing their hair, and painting their nails and –

> (**"Laugh"** *light on.*)

> (**HUNTER** *and* **FIELDER** *descend into rough-housing.*)

MARQUIS. Will you two quit it? Cut it out! They're looking at us.

HUNTER. So what? They're always looking at us.

MARQUIS. Then why don't they ever say anything?

HUNTER. Because they're waiting on us.

MARQUIS. Do you think Clementine heard I was in jail?

HUNTER. Pretty sure. Everyone has.

MARQUIS. Yeah. But I'm sure she doesn't think I'm dangerous. She's not like that.

HUNTER. Then why don't you go find out? Oh sorry. I know why. Because you're a pussy!

FIELDER. Meow!

MARQUIS. I am not!

HUNTER. Prove it then.

MARQUIS. How?

HUNTER. If you're so in love with Clementine, go talk to her.

(Blackout.)

Marquis in the Middle

(The quad at Achievement Heights Preparatory Academy. Brick and manicured hedges.)

(The **BOYS** *and the* **GIRLS** *stand on equal planes.* **MEADOW** *and* **PRAIRIE** *push* **CLEMENTINE** *toward* **MARQUIS**. **HUNTER** *and* **FIELDER** *push* **MARQUIS** *toward* **CLEMENTINE**.*)*

(The two meet somewhere in the middle.)

MARQUIS. Hi.

CLEMENTINE. Hey.

MARQUIS. Um...

CLEMENTINE. Yeah?

MARQUIS. Huh?

CLEMENTINE. Oh.

MARQUIS. What?

CLEMENTINE. ...

Selfie?

MARQUIS. Okay.

> *(***CLEMENTINE** *takes out her cell phone. The two pose for the picture.)*
>
> *(Just as she snaps the flash,* **TRU** *breaks in between the two.)*

TRU. Instagram?

CLEMENTINE. Totes!

MARQUIS. Tru?!

CLEMENTINE. Tru?

TRU. Thass me Boo. Wha's yo' name?

CLEMENTINE. Clementine.

TRU. Fo' real?

CLEMENTINE. ?

TRU. Like: Oh my darlin', oh my darlin' – I swear y'all got da whitest names ever, yo. Who is dis jump off?

MARQUIS. What?

TRU. *(Like a nerd.)* Your girlfriend?

MARQUIS. What?!... No... She's just my classmate.

CLEMENTINE. Just?

MARQUIS. No! My friend. We're friends...and classmates, but mostly friends.

CLEMENTINE. And who might you be?

TRU. I might be da best thing dat evuh happened to you.

MARQUIS. Don't mind him, he's just some kid I met –

TRU. Some kid? I'm not jus' some kid. I'm his cousin.

MARQUIS. My cousin?

CLEMENTINE. His cousin?

TRU. Yeah, on his muhvuh side. His real muhvuh side.

CLEMENTINE. You found your birth mother?

MARQUIS. No! He's lying. He's just some kid I met in jail.

TRU. Damn cuzzo, dat hurt. Dat hurt real deep. Here I am tryin' to strengthen our family bond, and you don' want nuffin to do wif me.

MARQUIS. We don't have a family bond.

         *(**CLEMENTINE** comforts **TRU**.)*

CLEMENTINE. *(To **MARQUIS**.)* Marquis, you should accept your birth family, you may have more of a bond than you think.

TRU. I tried to tell 'em, but will he listen to me?

MARQUIS. HE'S NOT MY COUSIN!

TRU. And she's not yo' girlfriend. Right?

CLEMENTINE. Well...no.

TRU. *(Smoooov.)* In dat case you can call me Mr. Debonair, all da pretty girls do.

CLEMENTINE. Okay...

TRU. Can I ask you a question? Favorite ice cream: Chocolate? Vanilla? Or Swirl? Me? I'm down wit' the swirl.

CLEMENTINE. I like Rocky Road.

TRU. Oh! So you a freak?

CLEMENTINE. ...

MEADOW. *(Calling.)* Clementine! C'mon, we've got to go.

CLEMENTINE. My friends are calling me. I have to go –

TRU. Not so fast, I'm tryin' to see what dat mouf do.

CLEMENTINE. My mouth?

TRU. Yes, yours snow mama.

CLEMENTINE. I'm confused. I'm just gonna go. It was nice to meet you Mr. Debonair. I guess I'll see you around.

TRU. I'll holla.

CLEMENTINE. Marquis...um, you should call me or something. Sometime.

MARQUIS. Sure.

> *(***MARQUIS*** and ***CLEMENTINE*** stare lovingly at one another as she exits with the other ***GIRLS.***)*

TRU. Oh my darlin', oh my darlin' –

TRU. *(Once they are gone.)* GODDAMN! Y'all got some top-grade high-quality snow at dis joint. Any one of dem THOTS could get it!

MARQUIS. THOTS?

TRU. *(Like a nerd.)* Those. Hoes. Over. There.

Tell me it's true what they say 'bout white girls?

MARQUIS. What do they say about white girls?

TRU. You know...

> (**TRU** *gestures.*)

MARQUIS. I –

TRU. Dat Clementine look like she DTF too. Yo! Hook a bruhvuh up!

MARQUIS. Well... I mean... I would...

TRU. Ooooh. I see. You got a thing fo' dat particular snow bunny, huh?

MARQUIS. What? No...

TRU. C'mon, yo. It's all over yo' face, she got your nose open so wide you could drive a Mack Truck through there. Honk! Honk!

> (**MARQUIS** *touches his nose.*)

Say no more. I'll back off. Give you a chance. Plenty of snow to go round. But word to da wise, she tryin' to feel some dick –

MARQUIS. God! Do you have to be so crass?

TRU. No.

MARQUIS. What are you even doing here?

TRU. Lookin' fo' you. You know you are one hard dude to find. You think bein' da only drop uh chocolate in da milk round here you'd be easy to single out – Wrong!

(**HUNTER** *and* **FIELDER** *begin inching toward*
MARQUIS *and* **TRU**.)

MARQUIS. Why are you looking for me?

TRU. I got some things for you. First off, I wanted to give
dis back to you.

(*He gives* **MARQUIS** *a book.*)

You was right. Dat Night-Cheze dude was on to some
real shit.

MARQUIS. You stole my book?

TRU. I didn' steal. I borrowed.

MARQUIS. You usually ask when you borrow something.

TRU. Yeah, but you don' usually give it back when you steal.

(**HUNTER** *and* **FIELDER** *crowd around them,*
perhaps a little too close.)

Can I help you two goon-ass muthafuckas?!

MARQUIS. Calm down, these are my friends.

HUNTER. Yeah, we're cool, homie.

TRU. Don' be sneakin' up on a nigga like dat. Y'all don'
know me, cuz.

HUNTER. My bad. My bad. Are we good, G?

FIELDER. (*At* **HUNTER**.) ...

TRU. Yeah we coo'. Lemme guess. Hunta. And Fielda.

HUNTER. I'm Hunter. Hunta F. Baby.

FIELDER. I'm Fielder.

TRU. Same thing. Anyways, can y'all get lost, I'm tryin' to
talk to my fam here.

HUNTER. Fam?

TRU. My cuzin.

FIELDER. You have a cousin?

MARQUIS. No, he's not my cousin. And anything you have to say to me, you can say in front of my friends.

> (**MARQUIS** *takes a step back in between* **HUNTER** *and* **FIELDER.** *They all have identical stances/postures.*)

TRU. Uh-oh. Marquis? Where'd you go?

> (**TRU** *pretends to look for* **MARQUIS.**)

> *(To* **HUNTER.***)* Marquis? Marquis? Is dat you?

> *(To* **FIELDER.***)* Or is dis you? Marquis?

> (**MARQUIS** *steps out.*)

Marquis! There you are.

MARQUIS. I don't get the joke.

TRU. You black as hell but you blendin' in with deese white muthafuckas. Y'all look alike. Y'all dress alike –

MARQUIS. It's a uniform.

TRU. Still, da way you stand, all entitled wit' ya chest pressed out. Walkin' like you got a pencil stuck up yo' ass. Thass why I had such a hard time findin' you. You turnin' white, yo.

MARQUIS. Whatever.

TRU. You a silver fox.

MARQUIS. Here we go. First I was wolf, then a wolfhound, now I'm a fox.

TRU. Nah, check it. See they doing dis experiment in Siberia on deese silver foxes. They call silver but they basically dark gray and black. They'd make nice-ass wintuh coat... Anyhow, deese scientists gotta bunch of wild ones and they put 'em in deese kennels and they started doin' experiments on 'em. Da scientists would walk up on 'em in they cage to see what da fox did. And they figured out dat da foxes did one uh two things: attack or try to escape.

MARQUIS. Fight or flight. Basic Psychology.

TRU. Right! But one in like every hunnid would do neither. And so da scientists would take dat tame fox and breed it wif another tame fox. And they repeated it, generation aftuh generation – breedin' only da tame ones, da ones dat wasn't aggressive or scared. And do you know what started happenin' to da black foxes?

MARQUIS. I'm sure you're going to tell me.

TRU. They started turnin' white, yo!

HUNTER. That's mad cray-cray, son!

FIELDER. *(At* **HUNTER.***)* Oh dear God.

TRU. It's true. They started barkin', and waggin' they tails fo' da scientists. And they turn white as Taylor Swift.

MARQUIS. Is this another one of your metaphors?

FIELDER. I don't get it.

TRU. I'm jus' sayin', one day you gonna wake up wif blue eyes and blonde hair.

MARQUIS. That metaphor is murky at best. The foxes are actually evolving.

TRU. Thass somethin' a ol' tame fox-ass nigga like you would say.

They ain't evolvin'! They bein' bred to please da scientists. A.k.a. da Man is decidin' what "good" qualities are. And in turn, da fox lose errything dat make dem a fox. They devolvin', nigga!

MARQUIS. I am so over this conversation. I'm sick of you insinuating that – I don't even know what you're insinuating!

TRU. I know. Thass the main reason I'm here. I'm gonna help you figure it out.

MARQUIS. Figure out what?

TRU. Figure out what you lost.

MARQUIS. I haven't lost anything!

TRU. Yeah…you have. Which is why I sat down over da weekend and wrote dis.

> (**TRU** *removes a stack of worn loose-leaf notebook paper from his backpack. He offers it to* **MARQUIS**. *He doesn't take it.*)

MARQUIS. What is this?

TRU. I've entitled it: *Being Black for Dummies*.

> (**TRU** *offers it to* **MARQUIS**.)

Go on take it. It's yours.

> (**MARQUIS** *takes it, apprehensively.*)

MARQUIS. What is all this?

TRU. A hunnid and fourteen pages of my wit and wisdom on what it takes to be a young black man in America.

MARQUIS. *(Reading.)* Number seventy-eight: "Always keep your head up, even if you're a crackhead." This is ridiculous!

HUNTER. Dude… I mean… Cuz, that look like hella more than a hundred and fourteen pages.

TRU. Oh. Thass cuz da last two hunnid or so is da complete and annotated works uh one Tupac Amaru Shakur. Cuz thass just, like, a prerequisite fo' bein' black.

MARQUIS. I don't need Tupac! I don't need any of this.

TRU. No...I think you do.

MARQUIS. No. I'm tired of you and everybody else telling me that I'm not "black" enough. Telling me I don't act "black" enough. Or talk "black" enough.

HUNTER. Well you kinda –

MARQUIS. ENOUGH! I don't need any of this. There is no set way to be black or act black. I can't not act black, because I am black, and so whatever I do is acting black. Or not. Or whatever! You, Tru, are a stereotype!

And I refuse to take lessons from some "homie" from the "hood" who thinks because he's from the inner city that he has the monopoly on "blackness." You are a joke! This is a joke! And you can take your manual and stick it – where the sun doesn't shine!

>   (**TRU** *takes the manual and searches for a particular page.*)

TRU. Numbuh thirty-one: "To make sure your point gets across, end all disputes with the phrase 'Bitch!'" Now had you had said, "...and you can take your manual and stick it – where the sun doesn't shine, BITCH!" I might've believed you. But you didn't know to do dat cuz you haven't read da manual.

MARQUIS. AAAAAAAAAAAAAAHHHHHHHHHHHH!

>   (**TRU** *gives* **MARQUIS** *back the manual.*)

>   (**MARQUIS** *lets the manual drop to the floor.*)

Just go away! Go Away! GO AWAY! –

>   (**MARQUIS** *storms off.*)

HUNTER. Bitch! He should have said it. Right there would have been a good spot too...

(*TRU chases after* MARQUIS.)

TRU. Where are you goin'? Yo' muvuh arranged fo' me to be yo' shadow fo' da day.

(FIELDER *exits after the two.*)

(HUNTER *is alone. He picks up the manual. It's the Holy Grail.*)

(*He shoves it into his backpack, then catches up with the rest.*)

(*Blackout.*)

After-School Special

(Marquis' bedroom. A glass ceiling.)

*(***MARQUIS*** *and* ***TRU*** *have glasses of milk and chocolate chip cookies the size of their heads.* ***DEBRA*** *stands at the door with a tray.)*

DEBRA. So Tru, what did you think of Achievement Preparatory Academy?

TRU. It was coo'.

DEBRA. Did you get along with the other boys?

TRU. Yeah, Hunta is coo'. Fielda coo'. Marquis was a little rude doh.

DEBRA. Marquis?

MARQUIS. What? I agreed to let you shadow me, even though I didn't want to.

TRU. But you kept tellin' people I wasn't yo' cuzin.

MARQUIS. You're not my cousin!

DEBRA. Marquis! Let Tru be your cousin.

MARQUIS. Whatever! It doesn't matter. It's just one day. One awful day.

DEBRA. Well, actually, I was thinking maybe it could be more permanent.

MARQUIS. What are you talking about?

DEBRA. Well, I think that having Tru around is good for you –

TRU. I do too ma'am.

DEBRA. And the idea of Tru hiding his light under the bushel that is the Baltimore Inner City Public School System won't allow me to get any rest at night. So, I propose, if Tru is amenable to the idea of course, that

I sponsor you in becoming a student at Achievement
Preparatory Academy –

MARQUIS. What?!

TRU. I don't know what to say –

MARQUIS. Say no!

TRU. You'd really do dat fo' me?

DEBRA. For you. For my son. And for your mother, who's
so burdened by responsibility she's grown, I dare say,
neglectful –

TRU. Now wait a minute –

DEBRA. I'd like to relieve her some of the guilt, frankly;
you will stay here through the week so that you may
attend school and you'll have supervised visitations
with her on the weekend.

TRU. Pump da breaks a second here. Don' get me wrong,
I'd love to go to Achievement Prep – they got all new
labs, and sushi in the cafeteria, and Wi-Fi...but I can't
see my muhvuh signin' off on dis.

DEBRA. Well if she doesn't have the foresight to give you a
better life and opportunities then I'll just have to make
her see.

TRU. What dat mean?

DEBRA. Don't worry, Tru. I have the law on my side.

TRU. Lissen, I gotta clear some things up, things ain't
exactly how you picturin' 'em –

DEBRA. You want to protect your mother, I get it. And trust
me, I'll do my best to keep things from getting...messy.
But you have to understand your future is paramount.
And I'm going to do everything in my power as an
apostle of the law to ensure it is bright and productive!

MARQUIS. Mom, this is insane! Did you run any of this by
Dad?

DEBRA. Your father doesn't control anything in this house!

MARQUIS. Mom –

DEBRA. You two finish your cookies. Don't worry, Tru. Mommy Debra is going to take care of everything.

>   *(**DEBRA** exits.)*

>   *(**TRU** starts after her. Stops. Paces.)*

TRU. Yo' moms is buggin', yo! Is she serious?

MARQUIS. Of course she is.

TRU. She can't call my muhvuh, man.

MARQUIS. Why not?

TRU. Cuz, she can't come at my muhvuh on some I'm gon' take yo' son from you type shit. She liable to get shot. My moms is ride or die, yo! We gotta think of somethin'.

MARQUIS. I've got an idea, you should do what I've been telling you to do the whole day: GO AWAY!

TRU. Naw, yo' muhvuh a coonhound, an' she got my scent up her nose.

>   *(**TRU** gets a text message. He takes the phone out of his pocket. Reads it.)*

>   *(Laughs. Texts back. Grins.)*

MARQUIS. What are you grinning at?

TRU. I just made a date wif Oh My Darlin' Clementine Perkins.

MARQUIS. YOU WHAT?!

TRU. Yup. Tonight. 8:00. At some bougie pizza place. It got four dolla' signs on Urban Spoon.

MARQUIS. You snake! You filthy slimy gutter rat!

TRU. Gutter rat? You mad or nah?

MARQUIS. Of course I'm mad! You know I like Clementine –

TRU. Actually, you are only just now confirmin' it –

MARQUIS. But you said you'd back off!

TRU. I did, I didn't say nuffin to her fo' two whole periods.

MARQUIS. You backstabber!

TRU. I'm sorry.

MARQUIS. Is that all you have to say? You're sorry?

TRU. Yes. I'm sorry I made da date with Clementine. But, if it's any consolation, I made da date using yo' phone.

(TRU tosses MARQUIS the phone.)

(MARQUIS reads the text messages.)

MARQUIS. So...wait. I...I have the date with –

TRU. Thass right! We gon' get you lost in da snow tonight. TURN UP!

MARQUIS. We?

TRU. Fasho. I gotta make sure you don' nut it up.

MARQUIS. You should be concerned with the hostile adoption my mom is drawing up in her office right now.

TRU. True. Fine, I can only take you so far. You sure you can handle dis on yo' own?

MARQUIS. ...

TRU. Fine, jus' remember dis one thing. I wanna say it's Numbuh forty-eight in da manual – you should really take a look at dat thing when you get –

MARQUIS. What? Remember what one thing?

TRU. Numbuh forty-eight, I think. "Any and all conversations with white girls, are always about your dick."

MARQUIS. How? How is that helpful?

TRU. You'll see.

MARQUIS. ...

TRU. Why are you just standin' around, Casanova? You need to get ready! Whatchu wearin'?

MARQUIS. This?

TRU. Yo' Young Republicans outfit?

MARQUIS. I wear this every day.

TRU. Exactly. And she see dat lame shit every day. You gotta do somethin' special to show her she special.

MARQUIS. Like what?

> (**TRU** *thinks. He goes to his duffel bag and removes the sparkly pair of Air Jordans.*)

TRU. You can borrow my Dorothies.

> (**MARQUIS** *thinks. He takes the shoes.*)

> (**MARQUIS** *exits.*)

You welcome! Douche.

> (*A beat.*)

Now... Oh Maamaaaaa Deeeeeeeb!

> (*Blackout.*)

Lost in the Snow

(A bougie pizza place. A glass ceiling.)

*(**MARQUIS** and **CLEMENTINE** sit at an intimate table with slices of pizza.)*

*(**MARQUIS** wears the Air Jordans.)*

CLEMENTINE. Wait! Don't take a bite. Put it back down.

MARQUIS. ...

*(**CLEMENTINE** arranges the items on the table just so. She snaps a picture.)*

CLEMENTINE. #foodpicsbruh.

MARQUIS. Oh, you're one of those.

CLEMENTINE. I am. Proudly. Besides your pizza looks so... unique. What's on it?

MARQUIS. My usual. Prosciutto, arugula, and goat cheese. What'd you get?

CLEMENTINE. Pepperoni.

MARQUIS. You must think I'm a weirdo.

CLEMENTINE. That's what I like about you.

MARQUIS. That I'm a weirdo?

CLEMENTINE. Oh. No. That you always defy expectations.

MARQUIS. What do you mean?

CLEMENTINE. Like, right now. Your pizza looks like a Barefoot Contessa recipe, and I order plain old pepperoni. Like, who'd expect that?

MARQUIS. What are you saying?

CLEMENTINE. Why do you look angry all of a sudden? Did I say something wrong?

MARQUIS. No. I'm just confused. This is my confused face.

CLEMENTINE. I'm not doing the best job of explaining either. Just know that it's a good thing. I really like you.

(They blush.)

MARQUIS. I...like you too.

(They blush harder.)

CLEMENTINE. Why?

MARQUIS. Why what?

CLEMENTINE. Why do you like me?

MARQUIS. Oh...I don't know...

CLEMENTINE. You should. If you say you like me, you should know why. I've already said one of the reasons why I like you.

MARQUIS. There are more reasons? Like what?

CLEMENTINE. Not until you say. You owe me one reason. Tit for tat.

MARQUIS. I guess...I like you because you're pretty –

CLEMENTINE. What else? I hope there's more than that.

MARQUIS. Tit for tat.

CLEMENTINE. Fine. I like you because you're smart.

MARQUIS. I like you because you're also smart.

CLEMENTINE. I like you because you're so...sophisticated.

MARQUIS. I like you because you stand up for people.

CLEMENTINE. I like your lips.

MARQUIS. My lips?

CLEMENTINE. You have really nice lips. Beautiful, full lips.

(They blush harder still.)

MARQUIS. I like your lips too.

CLEMENTINE. No. My lips are so thin. My mom says I can get collagen for my sweet sixteen.

MARQUIS. ...

CLEMENTINE. What?

MARQUIS. Nothing. I just didn't think you were that type of girl.

CLEMENTINE. What type of girl?

MARQUIS. The type that cared so much about her looks.

CLEMENTINE. I'm not –

MARQUIS. Not like that. I just meant, you don't seem to care about what people think. That's another reason I like you.

CLEMENTINE. I don't care what people think. It's mostly my mom's idea.

MARQUIS. Right... Your turn.

CLEMENTINE. Well...it's sort of hard to explain.

MARQUIS. I'm listening.

CLEMENTINE. Well, it's like... Okay, um... Remember how I was away all last summer.

MARQUIS. I heard you went to fat camp.

CLEMENTINE. It wasn't fat camp. It was Calorie Camp – and anyway that's beside the point. At camp I met these two girls, Ranesha and Ciara. They were both from the projects. No offense. But for whatever reason, we all just sort of clicked. And we did everything together. We were cabinmates, we did all our workouts together, and we shared secrets at night in our bunks. I told them things I wouldn't dare tell Prairie or Meadow. We were inseparable, or so I thought.

MARQUIS. What happened?

CLEMENTINE. Well, as much as we all shared, there was this one...word that Ranesha and Ciara used with each other that they didn't use with me. And it always seemed like a term of endearment, so one day I made the mistake of using that word, and man how they flipped. All of a sudden I saw a side of them I'd never seen before. They were yelling at me, and I tried to explain that I didn't mean any harm, but they kept yelling that I didn't understand, that I'd never understand, that I was incapable of "gettin' it." And in the end, they concluded that a friendship between people like us could only go so far. There was a wall, because we could never really understand one another. And I have never felt more white, than I did in that very moment.

MARQUIS. So...how does this relate to you liking me?

CLEMENTINE. Right. Well. Here you are. The antithesis. Proof that two people of different backgrounds can go beyond that wall. I feel totally comfortable with you. You and I are the same, no different. You never make me feel like I'm not "gettin' it." It's like...you never make me feel like I'm white.

MARQUIS. ...

CLEMENTINE. You're, like, one of us.

> (**MARQUIS** *is knocked back in his chair.*)

> (**CLEMENTINE** *and the pizza parlor are swept away.*)

> (*Enter* **DIONYSUS**. *Dressed in all white, with a bloody wound on his thigh.*)

> (**APOLLO** *enters. A hooded figure, dressed in all black.*)

MARQUIS. What's happening?!

DIONYSUS. Take off those Js. They're of no use to you. You don't know how to use them!

MARQUIS. Dionysus?

APOLLO. Keep tight inside of them. The magic must be very powerful, or else he wouldn't want you to take them off so badly.

MARQUIS. Apollo?

DIONYSUS. *(To* **APOLLO.***)* You stay out of this, or I'll fix you as well.

APOLLO. *(To* **DIONYSUS.***)* Rubbish. Be gone! Before someone drops a house on you too.

> *(***DIONYSUS** *cowers.)*

MARQUIS. There's no need to fight. I'll take them off.

> *(***MARQUIS** *attempts to remove the shoes.)*
>
> *(He can't.)*

APOLLO. You can no more remove the shoes than the Oriole can hide its orange plumes.

MARQUIS. I put them on. I can take them off.

> *(***MARQUIS** *tries again, futilely.)*

They're stuck! Here. Dionysus, help me take them off.

> *(***DIONYSUS** *attempts to remove the shoes but is electrocuted when he touches them.)*

APOLLO. He can't take them off either.

MARQUIS. I don't want them anymore. You can have them back.

APOLLO. You have accepted the shoes. They are not mine to take back. They are now your burden and your burden alone. You must accustom yourself to the weight of the secret. You do remember the secret don't you?

MARQUIS. I do.

DIONYSUS. But I...I thought I told you to forget the secret.

MARQUIS. I did.

APOLLO. You can't forget the secret.

MARQUIS. I haven't.

DIONYSUS. Then tell it to me.

MARQUIS. The secret is –

>   *(The words catch in his throat.)*

The secret is – I can't.

DIONYSUS. Tell me what the secret is!

MARQUIS. I can't think –

DIONYSUS. Unburden yourself. Let me shoulder some of the weight –

APOLLO. It's not your secret to carry.

DIONYSUS. Quiet you!

MARQUIS. Please. Dionysus. I don't remember.

DIONYSUS. But you just told him that you do.

MARQUIS. I can't explain it. When he asks I can. When you ask my mind goes blank.

DIONYSUS. So you don't want to tell me?

APOLLO. It is not his secret to tell. He can no more tell you the secret than a raven can teach its song.

DIONYSUS. Nevermore! You will tell me the secret or else –

>   *(**DIONYSUS** pushes **MARQUIS** back in his chair until he levitates parallel to the floor. **DIONYSUS** places a golden bucket next to his head. He places a white cloth over his face.)*

TELL ME!!

MARQUIS. I can't –

> (**DIONYSUS** *waterboards* **MARQUIS** *with a bottle of red wine.*)

(Drowning.) I don't. Remember. I can't. I can't say. It's right on the tip of my –

DIONYSUS. TELL ME!!

> (**DIONYSUS** *douses* **MARQUIS** *again.*)

MARQUIS. *(Drowning.)* Please! Please! Dionysus! Please! Apollo! Please!

APOLLO. I have given you the secret. You must acclimate to the restraint of it.

MARQUIS. I'll forget the secret. I'll take off the shoes. Please –

APOLLO. Never let those ruby sneakers off your feet for a moment –

MARQUIS. DIONYSUS! APOLLO! SOMEBODY! ANYBODY! HELP!

> (**DIONYSUS** *and* **APOLLO** *are swept away on a moonbeam.*)

> (**TRU** *enters in pajamas.*)

TRU. Nigga, wake up! Wake up!

> (**MARQUIS** *is in bed with the wine-soiled cloth over his face.*)

You interruptin' my rest. Heavy lies da head of a black man, let him get his rest when he can. Thass good – remind me to add dat to da manual.

> (**MARQUIS** *removes the cloth from his face. He now has blonde hair and blue eyes.*)

Oh shit son! I told you! I told you, you was gonna wake up white one day!

(**MARQUIS** *looks at himself in a hand mirror.*)

MARQUIS. I'm one of them now.

(*Blackout.*)

Lost in the Snow: Stutter 1

MARQUIS. DIONYSUS! APOLLO! SOMEBODY! ANYBODY! HELP!

> (**TRU** *enters in pajamas.*)

TRU. Nigga, wake up! Wake up!

> (**MARQUIS** *is in bed with the wine-soiled cloth over his face.*)
>
> (*He removes the cloth. He checks his face. It's normal.*)

You interruptin' my rest. Heavy lies da head of a black man, let him get his rest when he can. Thass good, remind me –

MARQUIS. Nevermind. It doesn't matter. You're here!

TRU. Fo' da time bein'. An' what of it?

MARQUIS. I want you to teach me.

TRU. ...

MARQUIS. Tru, I want you to teach me to be black. Where is the manual?

TRU. I'onknow. You had it last –

MARQUIS. I did not.

TRU. Yes. You did. I distinctly remember givin' it to you –

MARQUIS. And I gave it back to you.

TRU. You did not.

MARQUIS. I did too.

> (*An impasse.*)

Well can't you teach me without the manual?

TRU. I mean, I remember it – I wrote it. But we might miss some of da nuances. Dat shit was mad poetical, yo.

MARQUIS. I'm sure it'll be fine.

TRU. I'm sure it will be too. I jus' don' want it fallin' in da wrong hands. All dat wisdom could be tragic in da wrong hands.

    (Blackout.)

#1: In the Beginning

(**HUNTER** *stands alone with the manual.*)

[Projection: #1: In the beginning, there was the beat.]

(*The* **"Laugh"** *light stays lit for the duration of this scene.*)

(**HUNTER** *reads.*)

HUNTER. Number one: "In the beginning, there was the beat. It's an ancient beat going all the way back to the motherland, where they beat drums in bare feet and dance with titties free swangin. Find the beat. Keep the beat. It should be in every step you take, every move you make."

(**HUNTER** *tries to make a beat. It fails.*)

(*He tries again. It fails again.*)

(*He thinks. He turns his hat around backward.*)

(*He hears the far-off beating of African drums.**)

(*He finds the beat.*)

(*Blackout.*)

---

*A license to produce *Hooded, or Being Black for Dummies* does not include a performance license for any third-party or copyrighted music. Licensees should create an original composition or use music in the public domain. For further information, please see Music and Third-Party Materials Use Note on page iii.

#22: The City is Made for Niggas

(**MARQUIS** *and* **TRU**, *a glass ceiling.*)

[*Projection: #22: The city is made for niggas.
And vice versa.*]

(*A percussive rap beat being enacted by claps,
stomps, and slaps against the chest.*)

TRU. Thass it. You got it!

(**MARQUIS** *beams.*)

TRU. Okay, now less add some lyrics to dat shit.

MARQUIS. Lyrics? What lyrics? I don't know any lyrics –

TRU. Damn, calm down. We gon' freestyle.

MARQUIS. Freestyle?

TRU. Yeah, you jus' make it up as you go. You let da beat fill
you up and then you just say whass ever on yo' mind.

MARQUIS. I don't think I can do that.

TRU. Sure you can. It's easy. Watch. Drop da beat.

(*They begin the rap beat.*)

Check... Check...

MARQUIS. Check what?

TRU. Hush. Thass jus' whatcha say when you startin' up.

(*They begin the beat again.*)

Check... Check...
IN DA STREETS THEY CALL ME TRU, CUZ I SPIT DA
    TRUTH, HATERS CAN'T SNATCH MY SHINE, CUZ I BE
    BULLETPROOF / CHILLIN' IN DA BURBS, DIS SHIT IS
    SO ABSURD / BREAKIN' OUT DIS AREA, RUNNIN' WILD
    LIKE MALARIA / MY BOY MARQUIS WIT' ME, DIS NIGGA

A REPUBLICAN / HE LOST, BUT IT'S COO', HE GON'
LEARN TO BE A THUG AGAIN –

MARQUIS. Wait. Wait. Wait. I don't get it.

TRU. What's not to get?

MARQUIS. The rhyme scheme. The meter is off. You jump
back and forth between disyllable and trisyllables. And
is this supposed to hexameter or anapestic tetrameter –

TRU. Stop! You are completely overthinkin' dis, yo. First of
all, my trochees are on point. Second it don' matter! It
comes from here.

(*TRU gestures toward* **MARQUIS**' *stomach.*)

It comes from da gut. You plant yo' feet. Stand up tall.
Inhale. Exhale. And then say whatever pops in yo' head.

(*TRU begins the beat, slow and steady.*)

(*It goes on for several seconds without*
MARQUIS *saying anything.*)

What you waitin' fo'?!

MARQUIS. I don't know what to say.

TRU. Jus' say "check" a few times an' then let it rip.

(*TRU begins the beat again, slow and steady.*)

MARQUIS. Check... Check... Check... I...don't know what
to say.

TRU. Fine. Good. Use it. Thass it. Thass da first line, follow
it up.

MARQUIS. I don't know what to say, and maybe that's okay,
it's a pleasant enough day – No. No! I can't do this!

TRU. You right. You can't.

MARQUIS. Wait...don't give up on me just yet. I'm sure if
we kept –

TRU. I mean, you can't do dis here.

MARQUIS. Where?

TRU. Here. In Achievement Heights. It's like tryin' to teach a border collie to herd sheep in da attic. It ain't natural. We need to get into our element.

We need to be amongst our people. We need to stand on da pavement where da beat is indigenous.

MARQUIS. …

TRU. We need to go to Baltimore.

(Blackout.)

#32: Never Forget You Black

(**HUNTER** *stands alone with the manual.*)

(*Hat backward. Pants sagging. Stressed.*)

[*Projection: #32: Never forget you black.*]

(*The* "**Laugh**" *light stays lit for the duration of this scene.*)

(**HUNTER** *reads:*)

HUNTER.　Number thirty-two: "Never forget you black. At times you may forget, but remember that they never forget. It's better to remind yourself, than to have them remind you."

> [*Projection: #33: I repeat. Never forget you black.*]

Number thirty-three: "I repeat. Never forget you black. No matter what you doin', good or bad, be conscience that you a black man moving through space. Think about every word you say, every action you make, and judge that up against all the black men that ever was and ever will be. How do you look? Make adjustments if needed."

> (**HUNTER** *feels the stares of the audience closing in on him. They force him into a corner.*)
>
> (*He judges himself against all the black men that ever were and will be.*)
>
> (*He is given armor. Bling? A diamond grill? A durag?*)
>
> (*He is equipped.*)
>
> (*Blackout.*)

#87: Never Let a Nigga Catch You Slippin'

(**TRU** *and* **MARQUIS** *at a bus stop.*)

[Projection: #87: Never let a nigga catch you slippin'.]

(A glass ceiling.)

MARQUIS. Do we have to catch the bus?

TRU. How da hell else is we gonna get there?

MARQUIS. My mom subscribes to a sedan service. We could order one of those.

TRU. And we'll get jacked da moment we get out the car. We don' want dat kinda attention, yo.

MARQUIS. Wait. Where we're going, there's a possibility that we might get "jacked"?

TRU. There's always a possibility of gettin' jacked. The key is to not let niggas catch you slippin'.

MARQUIS. What do you mean, "slipping"?

TRU. Slippin'. Being unawares. Makin' yoself an easy mark. Niggas assess you real quick. They look fo' two things. What he got I can take? An' how easy would it be to take it? Cuz if a nigga thinks he can take yo' shine, odds are he will.

MARQUIS. I'm having second thoughts.

TRU. How come?

MARQUIS. Well, I'm pretty sure I look like I have something to take. And I'm pretty sure I look like it'd be easy to take it.

(**TRU** *assesses* **MARQUIS**.)

TRU. Yeah, you right.

MARQUIS. See? So let's turn back –

TRU. Naw. Jus' take off dat tie. An' here, you can wear my Dorothies again.

      *(**TRU** removes his shoes.)*

MARQUIS. What are you gonna wear?

TRU. I'ma rock dem slippery earls.

MARQUIS. Won't that make you a target?

TRU. I'm hood. No matter what I'm wearing.

      (They switch shoes.)

      (They walk in each other's shoes.)

And we can't walk around callin' you Marquis neivuh.

MARQUIS. What's wrong with Marquis?

TRU. Don't nobody go by they real name in da streets.

MARQUIS. Oh I get it. That way when the police are looking for you, no one knows your real name.

TRU. Your Borzoi is showin' again.

MARQUIS. It is not!

TRU. In da hood you get called fo' what you is. Yo' given name don' always fit, so da streets rename you.

MARQUIS. ...

TRU. ...

And it confuses da police.

MARQUIS. So, wait...Tru isn't your real name?

TRU. As far as I'm concerned it is.

MARQUIS. But it's not the name your mother gave you. What's your real name?

TRU. Thass none uh yo' damn business.

MARQUIS. Ooh. I bet it's something ghetto, like Daquan or Rayshawn.

TRU. Not even close, Mar-quis.

MARQUIS. Hey, it's my birth name. From my birth mother. The only remnant of the life I might've had.

TRU. Do you think 'bout dat a lot?

MARQUIS. What?

TRU. The life you mighta had.

MARQUIS. No. Do you?

TRU. Naw man. Naw.

MARQUIS. Oh look! There's the bus! There's the bus! –

TRU. Calm down. It's jus' MTA, it ain't a fuckin' golden chariot.

　　　　(Blackout.)

Helios

*(**HUNTER** stands alone with the manual.)*

(Hat backward. Pants sagging. He has a diamond grill in his mouth and a big, gawdy chain. More stressed.)

[Projection: #115: Avoid white women and their curiosities.]

(The **"Laugh"** *light stays lit as he reads and interprets.)*

HUNTER. *(Reads.)* Numbuh 115: "Avoid white women and they curiosities. They prolly see you as an 'experience.' Playin' in the snow can be fun, but don't let it consume you."

(He throws down the book.)

Damn yo! Iss hard out here fo' a nigga. Even the thots is out to get me. Where is da love, yo?

(He falls to his knees in despair.)

Heavy lies da head of a black man, yo!

(The **"Laugh"** *light begins to blink like a short circuit, until it dies completely.)*

*(**MEADOW** enters.)*

MEADOW. Hunter?

*(**HUNTER** nods "wassup.")*

I've been looking for you – You look different.

HUNTER. Do I?

MEADOW. Yeah. It's hot. Did you get a spray tan?

HUNTER. "Black people don't need spray tan." Numbuh seventy-seven.

MEADOW. Okay? If you say so –

HUNTER. I do say so. Bitch!

MEADOW. Excuse me?

HUNTER. Numbuh thirty-one: "To make sure your point gets across, end all –"

MEADOW. Hunter, you're acting weird. What's wrong with you?

HUNTER. I'm black!

MEADOW. Hunter, that's not funny.

>   *(She laughs.)*

What are you doing? Is this like, performance art?

HUNTER. I guess you could call it that. "Being a nigga is a performance piece." Numbuh eighty-nine.

MEADOW. I don't think you're allowed to say that word.

HUNTER. I'm allowed to say whatever da fuck I want. I'm black.

>   *(**MEADOW** surveys him.)*

MEADOW. Oh, I get it! This is like cosplay. You're, like, LARPing. I wanna play.

HUNTER. This ain't no game, be-yotch!

MEADOW. LOL. Okay, this is fun. So you're black?

HUNTER. Damn straight.

MEADOW. Am I still white?

HUNTER. Why wouldn't you be?

MEADOW. And you're still football captain?

HUNTER. Fastest nigga on the team.

MEADOW. And I'm still a cheerleader?

HUNTER. I guess.

MEADOW. But you're black?

HUNTER. Yes. For the millionth time, I'm a black man.

MEADOW. Okay. I'm into this. I can be like a Kardashian.

(She makes a Kardashian face.)

Hunta, you look good out there on the field.

HUNTER. Thank you, snow mama.

MEADOW. I love it when you take your shirt off. All that... dark skin and muscles. Sweating and glistening.

HUNTER. Is that a fact?

MEADOW. Yeah. I have a secret nickname for you...

HUNTER. What?

MEADOW. Helios.

HUNTER. Helios?

MEADOW. We used to have a horse in our stable. A breeder. An unmarked, true black stallion named Helios. I wasn't allowed to ride him; I wasn't even allowed to go near him. My dad had read that stallions couldn't control themselves around women. Apparently our smell drove them crazy. So he kept Helios under lock and key. But that just made me want to ride him more.

HUNTER. What da fuck this got to do wif me?

MEADOW. You know what they say, a girl's first love is her horse.

HUNTER. I don't know shit 'bout horses, yo. Numbuh thirteen: "Niggas don't ride horses."

MEADOW. Is it true...what they say...about black guys?

HUNTER. It depends on what they fuck said.

MEADOW. You know...about...

    (She gestures.)

HUNTER. Numbuh forty-eight: "Any and all conversations with white girls are always about your dick."

    (To **MEADOW.***)* I can show you better than I can tell you.

    (An invitation was all she needed. They begin to make out. Intensely.)

MEADOW. *(Coming up for air.)* This is weird. I'm like oddly turned on by this, but also sorta grossed out at the same time.

HUNTER. What the hell is that supposed to mean?

MEADOW. Sssshhhh....

    (They make out some more.)

    (At length:)

Oh... Oh... Oh Helios! Helios! Helios –

HUNTER. Stop!

MEADOW. What? What?

HUNTER. You can't be callin' me no damn horse, yo! That shit ain't sexy.

MEADOW. I'm not calling white Hunter a horse. I'm calling black Hunta a horse. Because the horse was black. It's a metaphor.

HUNTER. It's fucked up is what it is. I ain't no fuckin' show horse that you can just trot around. I'm a black man!

MEADOW. Okay... This is getting weird. You're taking it too far.

HUNTER. Too far?

MEADOW. Can't you just be white again?

HUNTER. Oh. So now that you have to deal with the real-life ramifications of a interracial relationship you ain't 'bout dat life. Typical.

MEADOW. Can't we just make out as, like, you and me?

> (**MEADOW** *goes to* **HUNTER.** *She tries to kiss him while pulling up his shirt. She notices a gun tucked in his pants.*)

Hunter? WTF! What are you doing with that?

> (**HUNTER** *draws the gun.*)

HUNTER. For protection.

MEADOW. Protection from what? We live in Achievement Heights.

HUNTER. It's hard out here fo' nigga like me. Gotta watch my back for crackas! Gotta watch my back for niggas! Can't let 'em catch me slippin'. I'm like some wild dog. If I beg and roll over and let the master scratch my belly, I gain his favor but the other dogs'll bite out my throat when the master ain't lookin'. On the otha hand if I growl and bare my teeth and howl I get respect from my people, but the master'll muzzle me and I can't eat. What's a black man to do? I gotta be two mufuckas. But how do I know when to be what? And how much? And what is the real me? Where do I begin? When am I myself? Being black is so complicated.

MEADOW. This isn't fun anymore. I'm just gonna go –

HUNTER. Wait! Don't go –

> (*He grabs her. Perhaps a little too hard.*)

MEADOW. Hunter let go! You're hurting me!

HUNTER. I'm sorry. I didn't mean –

>   *(They struggle against each other.)*

MEADOW. Hunter let go of me!

HUNTER. Just wait a second. I'll put the gun away –

MEADOW. Let go of me or I'm gonna scream –

HUNTER. Wait! –

>   *(**MEADOW** screams.)*
>
>   *(**HUNTER** lets go of her.)*
>
>   *(**MEADOW** nurses her arm for several silent beats.)*

MEADOW. You're acting like an animal!

>   *(She storms off.)*

HUNTER. Meadow come back. Meadow!

>   *(She is gone.)*
>
>   *(**HUNTER** is left alone with the gun.)*
>
>   *(He considers it.)*
>
>   *(Blackout.)*

Tru's Crib: Stutter 1

(Tru's house. Humble and meticulously clean.)

(A glass ceiling.)

(TRU *opens the front door. He pauses in the doorway, taking deep breaths. Savoring them.)*

MARQUIS. What are you doing?

TRU. What?

MARQUIS. You were just sniffing the air like a...basset hound.

TRU. ...

MARQUIS. What? I thought you liked dogs.

TRU. Whatever, yo. Stand right here. I'll be right back.

(TRU exits. MARQUIS surveys the room.)

MARQUIS. I like your house. It's very...clean.

(To himself.) Much cleaner than I thought it would be. Does that make me one of them?

(TRU returns. He tosses MARQUIS a hoodie.)

TRU. Here, put dat on.

(MARQUIS puts it on. TRU goes to him and tugs on his pants so they sag.)

Okay, now grab yo' balls and stand like this.

(TRU demonstrates.)

(MARQUIS adopts the pose.)

TRU. Coo'. Now, say, "Nigga."

MARQUIS. What? No.

TRU. Say it. It's part of yo' tutelage.

MARQUIS. No thanks. I don't like profanity.

TRU. Nigga, "nigga" ain't profanity. It's humanity.

MARQUIS. I don't like that word. I'm not even sure what it means. Like, sometimes you use it, and you're clearly describing a group of people that are a threat. Then sometimes you use it, and it's inclusive and you're a part of that group. Sometimes you say it like it's a term of endearment, and sometimes it's pejorative. Which one is it?

TRU. D. All uh dee above. Jesus man, you overthinkin' dis shit again. Sometimes niggas is good. Sometimes niggas is bad. Sometimes niggas is just niggas. Sometimes niggas is against you. Sometimes, niggas gotchyo back. Sometimes you don't know dem niggas. Sometimes dem yo' niggas. There's a nigga in all uh us. Even you. So...say it.

MARQUIS. N...no.

TRU. Say it or I'ma punch you in yo' mufuckin' mouf!

(He approaches **MARQUIS** *menacingly.)*

Say it, nigga.

MARQUIS. No.

*(***TRU** *shoves* **MARQUIS**.*)*

TRU. Say it! You a nigga, ain't you?

MARQUIS. No!

TRU. Yes you is!

*(***TRU** *shoves* **MARQUIS** *again.)*

MARQUIS. I get it. You're trying to provoke me.

TRU. You right. I am.

>   *(He shoves* **MARQUIS** *again, more forcefully.)*

Say nigga, nigga!

>   *(He shoves* **MARQUIS** *down to the floor.)*

MARQUIS. Stop shoving me!

TRU. Make me, nigga!

>   *(He shoves* **MARQUIS** *down to the floor again.)*

MARQUIS. QUIT shoving me. You're acting like a...

TRU. Like a what? Like a nigga?

MARQUIS. Yeah.

TRU. Then say it!

>   *(He tackles* **MARQUIS** *and pins him to the floor.)*

MARQUIS. Get off of me. Now!

TRU. Say it! I'm actin' like a what?

MARQUIS. GET OFF OF ME!

TRU. I'm actin' like a what?

MARQUIS. YOU'RE ACTING LIKE A FUCKING NIGGER!

TRU. Whoa. Whoa. Whoa. Whoa. Cut. Cut. Cut. Cut.

>   *(***TRU*** *releases* **MARQUIS** *and stands.)*

Nig-GA. Nig-GA. N-I-G-G-A. Not Nig-GER. E-R. Thass some white people shit, yo.

MARQUIS. That's not fair. I don't like this. I want to go home.

TRU. So you givin' up on being black?

MARQUIS. However you want to put it. I've had enough.

TRU. Fine. Go.

MARQUIS. ...

TRU. There's da door. You free to leave whenever you want. If you can find your way back to Achievement Heights from deep in da heart of da hood of Baltimore all by yo'self, den godspeed.

> (**MARQUIS** *goes to the door. He hesitates.*)

Wha's a matter?

MARQUIS. I don't know how to get back.

TRU. So you stuck? Feelin' a bit trapped?

> (**MARQUIS** *nods.*)

Good. Let dat sink in for a few minutes.

> (*Blackout.*)

Tru's Crib: Stutter 2

(Tru's house. Humble and meticulously clean.)

*(**TRU** opens the front door. He pauses in the doorway, taking deep breaths.)*

(Savoring them.)

MARQUIS. What are you doing?

TRU. What?

MARQUIS. You were just sniffing the air like a...basset hound.

TRU. ...

MARQUIS. What? I thought you liked dogs.

TRU. It's my muhvuh's perfume.

MARQUIS. ...

TRU. I don' see my muhvuh much. She workin' most days 'til midnight. When she get home I'm 'sleep. When I wake up she 'sleep. We constantly miss each other. She leaves fo' work at the exact time da school bell rings. But before she leave da house, she pause at the door, prolly doin' one last glance to make sure she ain't left nuffin. And her perfume sits here. And it say "Hello" when I walk in da door.

MARQUIS. That's sweet.

TRU. Shut da fuck up.

MARQUIS. No man, I mean it. You just dropped all the pretense in that moment. There's more to you than meets the eye.

TRU. ...

MARQUIS. Look I don't know if this thing is even working, but I really do appreciate you helping me out like this.

TRU. Don' get all soft on me, yo.

MARQUIS. No, I'm just saying, you're a cool dude.

TRU. So whatchyou sayin' is...I'm yo' nigga?

MARQUIS. ...

You my nigga.

TRU. My nigga!

> *(They embrace for a beat, then quickly realize
> what they're doing. They push off each other.
> **MARQUIS** punches **TRU** for good measure.)*

Can I ask you a question?

MARQUIS. ...

TRU. Am I da first black friend you ever had?

MARQUIS. No.

TRU. Really?

MARQUIS. Really. His name was Ernest. His parents were
white too. Our moms met at some adoption support
group.

TRU. I swear white people got support groups fo' everything,
yo.

MARQUIS. Yeah.

TRU. So. What happened?

MARQUIS. I don't know. We hung out a few times. Our
families celebrated Kwanzaa together one year.

But I don't know. It was always weird. It was like we
were both expecting to get something from each other,
but, like, neither one of us had it to give. But you are
the first to invite me into their home.

TRU. And how it feel?

MARQUIS. Oddly normal.

TRU. Coo'. Well make yoself at home. You want something to drink? We got Kool-Aid. I bet you ain't never had dat befo'.

(TRU *exits.*)

(**MARQUIS** *suddenly receives a text message. He reads.*)

(*He rereads.*)

(*He reads it again.*)

(**TRU** *returns with two glasses. He catches* **MARQUIS**' *expression.*)

Wha's wrong?

MARQUIS. Hunter.

TRU. *(Like a nerd.)* Hunter? What dat fuckboy done did now –

MARQUIS. He's dead.

TRU. ...

MARQUIS. He killed himself.

TRU. Shit...

MARQUIS. I gotta get back. Like, now. I'm gonna call a sedan, I don't care how that makes us look.

TRU. We don' need no sedan. You got any cash on you?

MARQUIS. Like twenty bucks.

TRU. Thass more'n enough fo' a hack.

MARQUIS. What's a hack?

TRU. A hood cab. A.k.a. jus' some nigga wit' a car. C'mon I'll explain it on da way.

(*They exit.*)

(*Blackout.*)

Headmaster Burns

(An interrogation room. A glass ceiling.)

*(***HEADMASTER BURNS*** *sits at one end of the table.)*

*(***OFFICER BORZOI*** *enters with* **MARQUIS** *in handcuffs.)*

OFFICER BORZOI. I got him sir. I picked him up getting out of an unregistered vehicle. There was another boy with him but...he got away.

HEADMASTER BURNS. We have the guilty party in custody, the other boy is inconsequential.

OFFICER BORZOI. Very good, sir.

HEADMASTER BURNS. That isn't to say that you shouldn't look for him. Put out an APB: Young black male. Considered dangerous.

OFFICER BORZOI. Yes, sir.

*(***OFFICER BORZOI*** *exits.)*

MARQUIS. Headmaster Burns, boy am I happy to see you.

HEADMASTER BURNS. Have a seat, Marquis.

*(***MARQUIS*** *sits opposite* **HEADMASTER BURNS.***)*

Can I offer you something to drink? Water? Coffee? Sweet tea?

*(***HEADMASTER BURNS*** *places an Arizona Sweet Tea on the table.)*

MARQUIS. No...thank you. What is this all about? I was headed to Hunter's house when we got pulled over –

HEADMASTER BURNS. Would you say that Hunter Chadwick was a friend of yours?

MARQUIS. My best friend. He and Fielder are my best friends.

HEADMASTER BURNS. Fielder Weitzman?

MARQUIS. Yes, Hunter and Fielder are my best friends.

HEADMASTER BURNS. That seems odd. Not more than an hour ago, Mr. Weitzman expressed the fact that his son Fielder is forbidden from communicating with you. Something to do with encouraging his son to cheat on a test.

MARQUIS. I didn't encourage him to do anything. They cheated off of me.

HEADMASTER BURNS. They?

MARQUIS. Hunter and Fielder.

HEADMASTER BURNS. Your alleged friends.

MARQUIS. No. Not alleged.

HEADMASTER BURNS. But Fielder was forbidden from fraternizing with you –

MARQUIS. True. But I –

HEADMASTER BURNS. It's funny you should use that word. "True."

MARQUIS. ...

> (**HEADMASTER BURNS** *removes the manual from a folder lying on the table. He flops it down.*)

You found the manual.

HEADMASTER BURNS. *Being Black for Dummies.* Is this yours?

MARQUIS. Yes... No... It was given to me –

HEADMASTER BURNS. By whom?

MARQUIS. Tru. He wrote it.

HEADMASTER BURNS. But I thought Tru was your pseudonym.

MARQUIS. No, Tru's a friend of mine. We met last week –

HEADMASTER BURNS. Where?

MARQUIS. ...

   (Enter **OFFICER BORZOI.***)*

HEADMASTER BURNS. Where?

MARQUIS. Here. I got arrested.

HEADMASTER BURNS. So you have a criminal history...

MARQUIS. No. We were trespassing...

HEADMASTER BURNS. We?

MARQUIS. Hunter, Fielder and me –

HEADMASTER BURNS. They were arrested too? That's news to me.

MARQUIS. No. They got away. We split off in three directions. I got caught. Ask him.

OFFICER BORZOI. I don't recall there being any other young men with you.

MARQUIS. What are you talking about? You saw us. We split up –

OFFICER BORZOI. I don't recall.

HEADMASTER BURNS. They were either with you and you were once again being a bad influence. Or they weren't with you and you're lying. Which one is it?

MARQUIS. They were with me –

HEADMASTER BURNS. So you were leading them astray, yet again. I see... Now, back to this salacious book. You are the author of it, correct?

MARQUIS. No. I told you, Tru wrote it.

HEADMASTER BURNS. Who is this Tru character? Is he your alter ego?

MARQUIS. No, he's real. I met him here last week. Ask him, he arrested him too.

OFFICER BORZOI. I have never arrested anyone named "Tru."

MARQUIS. Well, that's not his real name.

HEADMASTER BURNS. Then give us his real name, we'll find him and clear this whole matter up.

MARQUIS. I don't know his real name. But I met him here. My mom got him out. You remember, don't you Officer Borzoi?

OFFICER BORZOI. Legally, I can neither confirm nor deny –

MARQUIS. Nigga, what is your problem?!

(*Exaggerated gasp from* **HEADMASTER BURNS.**)

I'm sorry. I'm sorry.

HEADMASTER BURNS. Such profane language!

MARQUIS. If you back a fox into a corner, it's going to snap. I apologize for losing my cool.

(**HEADMASTER BURNS** *rifles through the manual.*)

HEADMASTER BURNS. Number eleven: "A black man is a fox. Don't get trapped. Don't let them back you into a corner, cuz when you bite they won't understand. They'll put you to sleep." Are you sure you didn't write this?

MARQUIS. I'm positive. It was Tru.

HEADMASTER BURNS. Your alter ego.

MARQUIS. No, he's my friend. He's real. He was with me tonight. You put an APB out on him. Young black male –

HEADMASTER BURNS. Considered dangerous. Do you often associate yourself with these types of people?

MARQUIS. Headmaster Burns, you know what type of people I associate with. You know me!

HEADMASTER BURNS. I know you have been a constant negative influence over the students of Achievement Prep.

MARQUIS. Constant negative influence? I'm president of the Positive Influence Club!

HEADMASTER BURNS. I don't see an Achievement Heights student here in front of me. I see a common thug. A wasted investment. We've done everything in our power to encourage and support you, but despite our best efforts you continue to misbehave and act in discordance with the accepted and promoted values of our fine institution.

MARQUIS. Sir, I –

HEADMASTER BURNS. This book fell into the wrong hands today, and it ultimately led to one of your so-called best friends taking his own life. And you are responsible. We are out of carrots, Marquis, or Tru, or whatever name you're going by these days. Now it's time for you to get the stick.

MARQUIS. What are you saying, sir?

HEADMASTER BURNS. You are hereby expelled from Achievement Heights Preparatory Academy.

MARQUIS. But Headmaster Burns –

HEADMASTER BURNS. And now Officer Borzoi will take over. I have done what I can to protect my school and its students. He will do his duty and make sure that the full hand of the law comes down on you.

*(**HEADMASTER BURNS** exits.)*

OFFICER BORZOI. Well, well, well...I knew when I let you go last week it wouldn't be long before our paths crossed again.

MARQUIS. It doesn't matter. Tru went to get my mom. She's on her way, and she's not going to let anything happen to me.

OFFICER BORZOI. I'm sure she'll be here huffing and puffing soon enough. Throwing her weight around. And you'll hide behind her whiteness once again. But your white bitch won't always be there. And every time you step a foot beyond the veil, there I'll be, on top of you like white on rice.

> (**OFFICER BORZOI** *exits, leaving* **MARQUIS** *alone with the manual.*)
>
> (*He reads from the back of the manual.*)
>
> (*He begins clicking his heels together.*)
>
> (*Unconsciously at first, then:*)
>
> (*The clicking gives way to a percussive rap beat.**)
>
> [*Projection: #202: Fight is Flight and vice versa.*]

MARQUIS. Black youth are seen as a problem. Inherently. And as a problem, they will seek to eliminate us. But we must fight and die...as NIGGAS. Not as the niggers that we've been taught to fear and hate. We must fight with the true knowledge of ourselves. Like Pac said in his infinite wisdom. Nigga stands for Never Ignorant

---

*A license to produce *Hooded, or Being Black for Dummies* does not include a performance license for any third-party or copyrighted music. Licensees should create an original composition or use music in the public domain. For further information, please see Music and Third-Party Materials Use Note on page iii.

Getting Goals Accomplished. Be who you are; but know who you are. Niggas, what are we going to do?

Fight or Flight? Fight and die if we must die. Or fly...

Like Niggas.

> (**MARQUIS** *closes the manual. The music stops.*)
>
> (*He thinks. He opens the sweet tea.*)
>
> (*He begins clicking his heels together again. Feverishly. Furied.*)
>
> (*The interrogation room dissolves into the darkness of night.*)
>
> (*Blackout.*)

Concerned Citizen

(**MARQUIS** *is alone.*)

(*Distant street lights. The glass ceiling is within arm's length.*)

(*Suddenly,* **CLEMENTINE** *emerges from the darkness. She hugs* **MARQUIS** *around the neck.*)

CLEMENTINE. ...

MARQUIS. Thanks for coming.

CLEMENTINE. Of course –

MARQUIS. I didn't know what to do. I tried to think of a safe place and I called you.

CLEMENTINE. I'm glad you did. It's all so terrible. I can't believe Hunter –

MARQUIS. Can we not talk about it? Any of it. I can't, okay?

CLEMENTINE. Okay.

(**CLEMENTINE** *hugs him again. They kiss.*)

(*They kiss some more.* **MARQUIS** *pulls away.*)

Finally.

MARQUIS. ...

CLEMENTINE. I've been waiting for you to do that for a while now. Word of advice, when a girl tells you she likes your lips that's an open invitation for a kiss.

MARQUIS. I'm not one of you. Okay? I'm different. We're not the same. And maybe you don't "get it" –

CLEMENTINE. But I –

MARQUIS. I'm not even sure if I "get it." But we are different. Not so different that we can't be girlfriend and boyfriend – But you can't like me just because I'm different. Or black. Or whatever. Because I'm more than that.

CLEMENTINE. I like you for you.

MARQUIS. Cool.

> *(They kiss again.)*

CLEMENTINE. Wait. Did you just ask me to be your girlfriend?

> *(They kiss some more.)*

MARQUIS. Your kisses taste like the rainbow.

> **(CLEMENTINE** *removes a bag of Skittles from her pocket.)*

CLEMENTINE. Take them from me. I tend to stress eat.

> **(MARQUIS** *takes the bag of Skittles.)*

> **(DIONYSUS** *enters, dressed as* **CONCERNED CITIZEN**. *He has a flashlight and a cell phone.)*

CONCERNED CITIZEN. What's going on here?

MARQUIS. Nothing sir.

CONCERNED CITIZEN. What are you two doing here?

CLEMENTINE. Nothing. We were just –

CONCERNED CITIZEN. Is he trying to hurt you?

CLEMENTINE. What? No? He's –

> **(CONCERNED CITIZEN** *shines the flashlight in* **MARQUIS'** *face.)*

CONCERNED CITIZEN. I know you. APB just came in over my police scanner app. Young black male. Considered dangerous. You stay right there.

> *(He takes out his cell phone.)*

CONCERNED CITIZEN. 911? Yes I've found that boy that ran off from the municipal office... Yes I'm looking right at him... Dark hoodie, like a gray hoodie. He's black... He's got his hand in his waistband.

MARQUIS. Sir, I –

CONCERNED CITIZEN. I can apprehend if you like... But he's right here... Fine. Yes we're on Story Book Lane... at the end of the cul-de-sac... Hurry. These assholes always get away.

CLEMENTINE. Sir, please. You've got it all wrong. He's my boyfriend.

CONCERNED CITIZEN. You don't know what he is. He's dangerous!

>   (**CONCERNED CITIZEN** *grabs* **CLEMENTINE** *and pulls her rather violently away from* **MARQUIS.**)

CLEMENTINE. Ouch! You're hurting me!

MARQUIS. Keep your hands off her!

>   (**MARQUIS** *takes a step forward.* **CONCERNED CITIZEN** *draws a gun.*)

CONCERNED CITIZEN. Don't come any closer. Hands up!

>   (**MARQUIS** *puts his hands up.*)

MARQUIS. Okay. My hands are up. Don't shoot.

>   (*The glass ceiling shatters.*)
>
>   (*Blackout.*)

Nebulas

(Nebulas. The twinkling and glinting of broken shards of glass surround.)

*(**MARQUIS** stands alone.)*

*(**APOLLO** appears. He whispers in **MARQUIS'** ear.)*

*(**MARQUIS** is washed in understanding.)*

APOLLO. Can you bear the weight of the secret?

MARQUIS. ...

(He shakes his head no.)

*(An army of hooded figures surround them. Welcoming **MARQUIS**.)*

APOLLO. There is no shame in that.

*(**APOLLO** begins to lead **MARQUIS** off. The hooded army moves in closer to them, until they are one with the mob.)*

(Indistinguishable.)

(Blackout.)

Epilogue

(A holding cell; implied bars, a bed/bench, a toilet/sink, a phone. A glass ceiling. The back wall is a projection of a bird's-eye view of the scene within the cell, broadcasting in real time.)

*(***TRU*** is sitting on the bench. ***NEW BLACK KID*** is lying face down on the ground, the hood of his sweatshirt pulled up over his head. Just beyond his hands are a bag of Skittles and an Arizona Sweet Tea.)*

TRU. What was you doin' again?

NEW BLACK KID. Marquising.

TRU. ...

NEW BLACK KID. *(Rising.)* You know, it's like Tebowing, or Planking, or Owling.

(Blackout.)

Epilogue: Nebulas

(A holding cell; implied bars, a bed/bench, a toilet/sink, a phone –)

(Nebulas. The twinkling and glinting of broken shards of glass surround.)

*(**APOLLO** appears.)*

*(**TRU** is washed in understanding.)*

APOLLO. Can you bear the weight of the secret?

TRU. ...

*(**"Laugh"** light on.)*

(Blackout.)

End of Play

www.ingramcontent.com/pod-product-compliance
Lightning Source LLC
Chambersburg PA
CBHW070333120726
47909CB00008B/2688